BOUND BY SECRETS

DEADLY ISLES SPECIAL OPS, BOOK 2

AMY MCKINLEY

ARROWSCOPE PRESS, LLC

Bound by Secrets

Copyright © 2021 Amy McKinley

(p) **ISBN-13**: 978-1-951919-03-0

(e) **ISBN-13**: 978-1-951919-00-9

Publisher: Arrowscope Press, LLC; www.arrowscopepress.com

Editing— Kate B., Line Editor, Virge B., Proofreader, Red Adept Editing

Cover Design—T.E. Black Designs; www.teblackdesigns.com

Author photo provided by—Brookelyn Anhalt of lovely.life.photography; https://www.facebook.com/LovelyLifePhotography-102253596490708

Interior Formatting & Design— Arrowscope Press, LLC; www.arrowscopepress.com

---

KAYLA

My mind was made up. I was leaving Roy, and there was nothing he could say to stop me.

My outrage snapped and crackled with each step as I paced in front of the large flat screen, blind to the wall-to-wall windows highlighting the azure ocean off the Ala Moana Beach. The too-real images on the sports channel mocked me, playing highlights of his fight. The match was spectacular, and he'd won by a knockout in the third round. The blonde on his arm, the one caught on camera with her tongue in his very willing mouth as he'd left the stadium, wasn't.

I'd believed him when he'd told me how much I meant to him—I'd even moved in with him. I thought the four months we'd spent dating meant something—specifically, monogamy. It hadn't.

The sound of the lock tumbling and the whoosh as the door opened told me he was home. An avalanche of rage fueled me as I stomped across the wooden floor in the condo I shared with him, intercepting Roy seconds after he entered the living room. The image of him kissing then walking out of the arena with one of the numbers girls played on repeat in my mind. I had been warned about him. I should have listened.

We stood toe to toe, and I tilted my head back to take in the behemoth size of the heavyweight champ while the lingering scent of sweat, blood, and another woman's perfume washed over me. His pursuit of me, the overwhelming gifts, and all the sweet moments we'd shared fizzled to nonexistence, and I questioned how much I knew him in the aftermath of one fateful evening. Mouth pinched in a tight line, I crossed my arms and waited.

A wide grin stretched his handsome but battered face. "You should have been there. It was spectacular."

"I watched your fight." *Did he think I wouldn't?*

When he went to touch me, I spun around, putting some space between us. "Why? Why should I have been there, when you had all the company you needed? I saw you tonight, Roy. I saw *her*."

Unblinking, he crossed his mammoth arms over his chest and glared. "Think before you say something you'll regret."

"Threats?" My voice rose an entire octave, and I waved my hands around. "Are you kidding me? You kissed one of the numbers girls. You left with her glued to your side. And I'm supposed to watch what I say?"

There was a loud crack. My head whipped to the side. My body helplessly followed the momentum while agony burst through the left side of my face. I landed in a heap on my side. I hadn't seen it coming. He'd moved too quickly. That was why he was the undefeated champ, who'd won another title hours earlier.

Before I could get up, his fingers dug into my hip, forcing me to turn to my back. Then he straddled my body, looming over me.

I tasted true fear.

His hand closed around my neck, and he applied pressure. Panic sizzled through me, and my eyes went wide.

"I see the honeymoon is over," he rasped through swollen, split lips. "Let's get one rule straight. You don't get to complain."

His brown eyes were cold, hard, and as unyielding as the rest of his title-winning body. I bucked against him with no success. *How did I not see this coming?* His wandering eye was well known, but he'd been so sweet to me—until now.

"You're my girlfriend, living in my home, and you'll do what I say." He squeezed, applying more pressure.

My access to air was minimal. I thrashed underneath him.

He whispered in my ear, "There are rules to follow. The most important to remember is that I own you."

Through the haze of terror, his words hit home like the unyielding steel of a jail cell door slamming.

Black spots crowded my vision as I sucked air through a constricted windpipe, desperate to fill my lungs. A wave of dizziness vied with intense fear. My hands curled around his wrists, nails embedding into his skin like claws. Tingles spread all over me. My muscles weakened then went slack. I felt weightless despite the heavy man over me. My dead-weight arms flopped to my sides, and the world faded a little more.

There was no air. Sheer panic morphed into the horrifying realization that I would die.

Awareness slowly trickled back in. The dark void I was in grew lighter, and shapes formed. I didn't know how long I'd been lying there. My body was both weightless and heavy. Light gradually filtered back, as did Roy's voice from somewhere other than directly over me. Although painful and raw, there wasn't anything crushing my throat. He wasn't on top of me. But I wouldn't let that detail lure me into a false sense of security. I didn't move, didn't alert him to the fact that he hadn't killed me. Maybe he'd meant only to bring me to the brink of death.

Whatever his intentions were, they were bad enough for me to know I had to be careful in my escape. As I lay there, plotting, I tried to pick up as many clues as possible about who he was talking to and whether he was leaving. We had a balcony off the living room, but we were up too high. I couldn't leave that way. It would have to be the front door.

The longer I remained on my back, the more the dizziness receded. My mind whirled, and my muscles twitched with the desperate need for action.

The door slammed, and I was instantly on my feet, moving through the living room to our bedroom. I yanked the closet doors open, heaved my suitcase onto the bed, ripped my clothes from the hangers, and haphazardly stuffed them inside. Next, the bathroom. Everything went into small garbage bags I found under the sink. If I ended up leaving something behind, I wasn't coming back.

I settled my oversized purse on my shoulder and went from room to room, filling it and my arms with anything that was mine. I was almost out of there. With my suitcase packed and rolling behind me, I paused at the entrance to the office. I swallowed painfully then went to the desk, pulled the drawers open, and riffled through the contents. *There!* I palmed the flash drive with the Honolulu Star-Advisor logo then slipped it into my pocket. I tore through the condo on winged feet, passed through the entrance, and, once the elevator arrived, got inside.

My death grip on my suitcase didn't ease as the floors ticked away with each muted ping. I locked down the muscles in my shaking legs as best I could when the elevator softly thumped to the garage floor, bypassing the lobby entrance all together. The last thing I needed was to exit where there were bound to be people, possibly press, and draw attention to myself.

With a whoosh, the doors retracted, and I stepped over the threshold, my suitcase bumping along behind me. My flip-flops clapped against the marble floor, and I ducked my head as two residents made their way to the elevator I'd just vacated, their chatter like a spike driving through my skull to the beat of my pounding headache.

Tears streamed down my face. With each swallow, my throat felt like I'd ingested shards of glass. My hardtop Jeep was two cars away. I hurried over, hit the unlock button, and threw my belongings inside.

Roy had a small storage unit in the garage not far from where I parked. He'd given me the combination, as I frequently went in and out with my surfboard. If I didn't think I had the time, I would have left it, but I'd caught a couple of words from the phone call. It'd sounded like his agent, and I guessed he was meeting him somewhere. Maybe another press opportunity.

Whatever it was, I didn't care, so long as I was able to get away from him. I jogged over to the locked units along one side of the wall, moving to the unit marked as his. With practiced ease, despite my trembling hands, I got the board out, returned the short distance to my car, and secured it on the roof rack.

I climbed inside, buckled up, and pressed the start button. The engine turned over, accompanied by the sense of freedom rushing into me. I threw the Jeep into reverse, backed up, then got the hell out of there.

My windows were down, and the humid Honolulu air rushed in, whisking away my tears and drowning out the sound of my sobbing. I wanted to put distance between us but couldn't go home—not yet. I figured I would be safe for at least one night. My car ate up the miles despite the evening traffic. I needed somewhere to sleep. Tomorrow, I would move again.

After a couple of hours of sleep and with ice on all the places he'd bruised, I would be able to function again. Because there was no way I would make it easy for him to kill me, leaving my parents to bury another one of their children.

KAYLA

One week later

I was in dire need of caffeine but stood on the sidewalk in front of the Coffee Hut, held prisoner in an endless stream of small talk with one of my parents' friends, Mrs. Simon. As people came and went through the entrance, many with to-go cups, my mouth salivated. The rich aroma of the beans wafted my way from inside. Resolved, I toughed it out and chatted, hoping for a break so I could excuse myself and feed my morning addiction.

In a slow ascent, the sun's rays chased the early-morning chill from the Honolulu air. I sensed the conversation coming to a point where I could extract myself when all the fine hairs on my body stood at attention. I felt, rather than saw, someone watching me. Fear skated along my spine. Although I was somewhat aware that it wasn't Roy, that didn't register with my fight-or-flight readiness. I sucked in a breath, interrupted our conversation with some excuse, and said goodbye.

On the balls of my feet, I pivoted, tense and ready to run,

and almost dropped to my knees as desire hit me at the sight of the only man I'd ever loved. Or wanted.

Fortunately, reality slammed into me, and I scowled. I had to have been delusional. I hadn't seen Jaxon Hale in years, and judging by my last relationship, I probably shouldn't have trusted myself. *What did I know about love when I was a teenager?*

"Hey, Kayla." His deep, commanding voice wrapped around me like a lasso, and I took an involuntary step forward. My mouth watered at the sight of my high school crush, holding a to-go cup of much-needed coffee. I tore my gaze away and audibly swallowed. *I can do this.*

A week had passed since the incident with Roy, enough time for the swelling and majority of the bruises to fade. But going home wasn't an easy decision, and I hadn't counted on running into him. Even though I'd run into his brother, Xander, at the beach, surfing with friends during one of my visits to see my parents, I thought I would somehow be able to avoid Jax.

Jaxon was many things: my brother's best friend, my kryptonite, and all my firsts—until he failed us both.

I fought through my lustful gaze, tilted my chin defiantly, and returned the hello through clenched teeth. No matter how much I loathed him, I could feel his touch from all those years ago. No one had ever been able to surpass how he'd made me feel. And God help me, I still wanted him.

I squared my shoulders and let the anger and pain from that night rise like a shield around me. "I heard you were working for my dad."

"For now. Xander mentioned that he saw you at the beach with some friends. His favorite part of running into you was hearing that you had a new nickname for me."

Oh, right! A burst of laughter made it past my lips. I so needed that. "Yeah, Jackass. It fits, doesn't it?"

If I hadn't known Jax so well, I would have missed the tightening of his mouth and flash of pain in his deep-brown eyes.

But that couldn't have been real. He held no remorse for abandoning Kieran and me when we'd needed him most.

"Where've you been? I would have thought you'd be here for your dad's surgery."

"I was." I barely held back the growl, but it cost me, and my voice shook with it. "I came for the first few days then had to get back for work." I cringed at the lie, but he didn't need to know I'd gone back because of Roy. "I'm here now."

His eyes skimmed me from head to toe and back again. I took a step forward, done with our meaningless talk and in dire need of caffeine. When I neared the door—and him, because he was leaning against the brick between the large front window and the entrance—his hand shot out and lightly grasped my arm.

I jerked at the touch, which made traitorous heat pool low in my abdomen, and snapped, "What are you doing?"

"Don't go yet, Kayla. It's been a long time, and it would be nice to catch up. Can I get you a cup of coffee?"

I wasn't going to get away as quickly as I'd hoped, but coffee would help. "Carmel latte, please."

He went inside, and I settled on one of the wrought iron chairs around the few tables crowded on the sidewalk near the window. I didn't want to go inside, as I suspected the walls would feel like they were closing in on me. I was glad I'd worn a stretchy short-sleeved T-shirt and yoga pants. A long-sleeved high-neck shirt would have been preferable, but I didn't anticipate seeing anyone, as Honolulu was a big and busy city. I should have realized that I would know someone at the Coffee Hut, as it was a favored place for people I knew.

My parents had kept me informed about Jaxon, even though I'd told them I didn't care. They liked to tell me, when I visited, that he was still single. Fortunately, he'd been on missions with the Navy many times, and the likelihood of an encounter had been slim to none—but not anymore.

Nervous, I crossed my legs, bouncing the top one and then pulling my hair forward, so it covered as much of my neck as looked natural. Even though the bruises were fading, I'd caked on makeup to ensure they weren't noticeable.

I jumped when the door opened, and Jaxon came out with my coffee in an extended hand. Grateful, I took it and tentatively sipped the liquid. It was hot. I pried the lid off then blew on it, willing it to cool faster so I could infuse the life-altering caffeine into my body.

He took a seat across from me and leaned back in his chair. His eyes were observant, his body deceptively relaxed. I'd seen him go from that pose to immediate action. There was nothing about Jaxon that wasn't lethal, especially to my heart.

Beneath my lashes, I studied him further. The decade we hadn't been in contact had been good to him—he was more handsome than ever. Athletic and muscular, he'd always turned heads. It was easy for a woman to get lost in the penetrating gaze of those warm brown eyes, which saw more than we ever wanted him to. The crescent scar over his left eye begged for my finger to trace it. He exuded power. The night we'd shared, then the betrayal, hung in a heavy, unspoken silence between us.

"Will you be staying long?" He took a drink of his coffee then set it on the table.

"As long as I'm able. I'm headed to my parents'… just stopped for this." I lifted the drink in a mini salute then took a sip of heaven in a cup. A gust of wind whipped by, blowing my hair away from my face. His gaze followed my every move, the intensity of it like a live wire, and I sighed. He didn't understand why I was gone, and I wasn't about to tell him, but maybe I could satisfy some of his curiosity, throw him off the trail. "Just ask whatever you're thinking."

"Tell me about the bruises." His voice was whisper-soft, but I knew that was when he was his most dangerous.

My spine snapped straight, and in my mind, I looked back to

when I'd put the makeup on, examining every inch of my face and neck. I'd covered it all. *How does he know? Did I rub some off while I was talking with Mrs. Simon?* "What are you talking about?"

"You've never worn that much makeup before—"

"Maybe that's because we haven't been around each other since high school. Specifically, the night we were together. Not even at Kieran's funeral. So how would you know how much makeup I wear?" I countered.

A sad half smile curved his mouth. "Because I know you. And there are also faint shadows beneath the makeup on your neck. I suspect there are more. What happened?"

I stomped down on the panic before it could take over. I was safe. He couldn't have known. Then my eyes narrowed at the obvious way he'd ignored my digs about when we'd stopped talking. "I had a run-in with my board when I was surfing last week." I offered a chilly smile that didn't encourage further questions. "It's nothing."

His phone beeped, and he broke eye contact to glance at the screen. A fierce frown marred his face, and I couldn't stop the stab of concern. I hadn't talked with Xander for long that day at the beach, but I assumed both he and Tyler were still in the Navy. Whether his brothers were okay or not had to have been a constant worry for Jaxon since he was out.

"What is it?" Before I could stop myself, I reached out and covered his hand. He flipped his over so that his palm was against mine then laced our fingers together. It was a simple touch, but it meant everything to me. And my traitorous heart sped up at the realization.

When his troubled gaze met mine, I knew I would do whatever it took to help him. I would even bury my hurt and betrayal over the circumstances of our lack of communication over the years.

"It was a news alert. Several explosions happened at the same time."

A mask fell over his features, hiding his troubled expression, and I leaned forward and placed my hand on his tense forearm. Jaxon wasn't built like most men. He was a warrior, a SEAL, former or not. He had an innate moral code to defend, to save. And while he didn't say it, we were both thinking the news alert he'd mentioned was possibly a terrorist attack.

He stood and pulled me from my chair, drawing me close. When he wrapped his arms around me, and I rested against his solid chest, I felt safe for the first time that week. We had our differences, too many to count, but maybe there was a way he could help me without me telling him what happened. I wound my arms around his waist and offered him the same comfort he'd given me as an idea of how he could help me formed.

3

JAXON

Kayla and I parted ways soon after I got the alert on my phone. She climbed into her Jeep to go to her parents' house, and I got in the squad car and headed for the station. I'd wanted to grill her over what was going on, especially after she'd all but admitted that my guess about the bruising was true. It had been more than a guess, actually—the side of her neck was tinged green, and I saw it when the breeze blew her hair back. The discussion wasn't over. I knew where to find her.

The sound of the phones ringing and conversations vying to be heard enveloped me as I stepped inside the station, along with the scent of coffee. I shifted into work mode, promising myself I would see her soon.

Several officers crowded around a TV airing a repeat of the three explosions caught on pedestrians' video. Fiery flames consumed the front portion of a floral shop and a car in front of a breakfast joint, and a third video captured the aftermath of a residential explosion. Only the homeowners' names had been released so far. With the unrest in South America, my mind pinpointed a potential militia group responsible for the American deaths. There had to have been a connection.

"Matheson"—my gut screamed to get involved in the investigation and that I was missing some vital piece of information that would tie it all together—"who's the detective on this?"

He let out a gusty breath before heading back to his desk, tossing a name over his shoulder before he sat: "Nolan."

"Has any more information come through on the victims?" I tore my gaze from the horrifying images on the screen to comb the station, looking for the lead detective, who resented my presence and close connection to the chief.

Nolan and I didn't get along on the best of days—he inaccurately thought I was gunning for his job. I pressed Matheson for details, and fortunately, he complied. "The residence belonged to the Greers. Both were inside, and neither made it. We don't know yet about the florist. If they've found anyone, I'd imagine they're waiting to inform family first." His chair groaned under his weight, and he bent his head to two-finger type whatever report he was working on. "The only evidence that I know of was a gas-company truck parked on the curb outside the residence yesterday. Nolan would have more details."

I grunted. Nolan wouldn't share information with a beat cop he harbored distrust for, even if his so-called reasons were far from the truth. I couldn't wait to turn in my badge and get on with my next endeavor.

My cell phone rang, and I moved to a relatively quiet corner of the station to answer when Xander's name popped up on the screen. He and Riley were still on their honeymoon in the Cook Islands and not due back for a few weeks. "Hey."

"Jax." The sound of lapping water surrounding their overwater bungalow filtered through the line along with Riley's "hello" in the background, which I reciprocated. "We caught some footage of the explosions. Know anything?"

I rubbed a hand across my forehead. "No. Have you checked in with Tyler?"

"He's not back yet, so no."

"The timing's shit." We couldn't talk about what was going on with the mission Ty's SEAL team was on—neither of us had re-upped. I could have fought my honorable medical discharge, but I hadn't. It had been time for a change.

We knew enough from being in the Navy. Especially Xander, as his return to civilian life was recent.

"I'm worried about Ty," he said.

I was too. "I'm going to put a call into Jack, see if he has any intel." Jack Davis ran a team of former SEALs who did mostly rescue and recovery missions. He was a friend, and I would soon join his company's ranks on an as-needed basis. Xander too. Jack had CIA and fed connections who could have relevant information.

Water splashed in the background, and I figured it was Riley jumping off the deck, into the lagoon. "Keep me informed."

"Goes without saying." I could sense Xander's grin without having to see him. Not much would have gotten him to call during his honeymoon. But a possible terrorist attack, especially one that coincided with our baby brother on a mission to South America, did. "How are things with Riley?" My new sister-in-law and I hadn't met under the best of circumstances. She'd been the victim of several break-ins, and we'd almost lost her at one point. I hadn't been a fan at first. The friction had been because I'd been so worried about my brother when Riley was the focus of the suspicious incidents, but that was over, and Xander loved her. She was family, one of us now, and I couldn't have been happier for them.

"Riles took about a billion pictures just this morning." Contentment bled from Xander's voice. "We're going snorkeling later today then on a party boat. Three weeks isn't long enough. We're doing all the cliché tourist things that I swore I never would. But man, I get the appeal by her reactions alone. How the hell did a week pass already?"

We had our own piece of paradise on the island our family

owned, but it wasn't the same as getting away. Xander and Riley deserved it. She hadn't done a lot of traveling. She was the perfect partner for my brother and fit right in with the rest of us too.

I couldn't help thinking about Kayla joining our expanding family. I'd wanted her when we were younger, and I wanted her still.

4

KAYLA

After Jaxon left to go to the police station, I got behind the wheel with my to-go coffee. It was early, but I knew my parents would be awake. Even though it was risky, I needed to see them.

I hadn't expected to run into Jaxon so soon or to have the memories of our only night together crowd my mind. In person, I couldn't fight the images or the magnetic attraction that had always existed between us, even when we were miles or continents apart. How I felt near him and linked through our past didn't matter—he'd betrayed my brother and me. I'd moved on.

I inched through the traffic, thick with people rushing to work, and realized I had to alter my way of thinking if I wanted to keep my parents safe and make it harder for Roy to find me. As a professional fighter, he had the stamina and zealous devotion to see things through when he put his mind to what he wanted. I only hoped he didn't want me back as badly as I feared he did.

Twenty minutes later and out of the crush of commuters, I

wove through the neighboring streets then pulled to the curb in front of my childhood home. I had another sip of my lukewarm coffee and took a moment to enjoy the tropical plants, the bay window, and the walkway.

I left my luggage in the backseat and climbed out. It was a quaint neighborhood with immaculate lawns and pretty flowerbeds that ran the length of the house. Mom kept everything weeded and beautiful, while Dad maintained the lawn. Hot pink, fuchsia, purple, and a wide array of green leaves were a tribute to Mom's capable gardening skills.

My gaze tripped over a sign in the yard that hadn't been there before. *What the hell is that?* I couldn't quite believe it and climbed out to take a closer look as I made my way up the driveway. *They're selling the house?*

Denial and devastation at the thought of losing another connection to my brother weighed heavily in my heart. I staggered to the front door and leaned against the brick, taking a moment to corral my ping-ponging emotions.

There had to have been an explanation, and I vowed to listen to it with a calm mind, even though I wanted to scream at them not to sell our home, the place where my brother and I had created so many memories. But I couldn't—Dad's heart surgery was a bigger fear. The idea of causing him distress wasn't a good one. He needed to fully recover because I couldn't lose him too.

Wiping any traces of what I was feeling from my face, I rapped my knuckles on the door before using my key to enter. "Aloha."

Hibiscus intermingled with the lemony smell of furniture cleaner, both familiar and heartwarming. They symbolized home and were a comforting scent from my past.

"Kayla!" Mom shrieked as she rounded the corner and pulled me in for a hug. "I didn't know you were coming." She patted my cheek, smiling from ear to ear. "Come to the kitchen. We have a coffee cake I pulled out of the oven ten minutes ago, and your father is in there, drinking decaf." Her voice hushed to a conspiratorial whisper.

My eyebrows rose practically to my hairline. "How did you manage that?" Dad was a coffee addict like I was. We snubbed decaf.

She smirked. "I told him it was a new flavor. I kept the decaf part to myself."

"That's downright evil." I grinned back at her while making a mental note to check what coffee pods were the decaf ones so she didn't pull that trick on me too.

I followed her, resisting the urge to tug on one of the strands of her wildly curly hair, which fell just past her mid-back. When I was young, I used to do that, fascinated by how her curls would spring right back into the corkscrew shape they were always in.

We were the same height, mirror images of one another minus wavy hair against her curls and despite the age difference and the few extra pounds Mom carried, which made her all the more beautiful. We'd grown closer since Kieran died. He was her angel, and I was the apple of my father's eye.

Things had changed after that night—more than love and family bound the three of us. We were tied together in grief and survival, relying on each other to stay afloat. We'd done a pretty good job of it, too, except for my recent relationship with Roy, which I hoped they never found out about.

We entered the kitchen, arm in arm. Dad sat at the round table with a steaming mug and plate with fruit, eggs, and a small slice of coffee cake. "Aloha, Dad."

When he turned, I fought overwhelming emotion and sheer relief at seeing him so hale after a week of rest and recovery. I bent and gave him a gentle squeeze and was swallowed in his embrace. "You look wonderful."

And he did. Dad was half Samoan, while Mom was not. He

was big and muscular, and other than the small pouch from Mom's fantastic cooking, he looked like a linebacker, with the tribal tats to match. Mom was the opposite, with her light skin, green eyes, and petite build. Kieran and I had the same eyes and smile, which we got from Mom. That was where the similarities ended. Kieran had been a replica of our dad, while I was Mom's.

"Sit." Mom motioned for me to take the chair across from Dad, so I released him and straightened. She already had a plate piled high with breakfast, and I did what she said and dug in.

"You're too thin, Kayla." Mom fluttered around, replacing my cold coffee with a fresh mug. I narrowed my eyes at her, and she shook her head, letting me know it wasn't the same as what dad had. "Have you been skipping meals?"

I waved away the concern that etched lines around her mouth, despite the fact I truly hadn't been eating much for the past week. "I'm fine. I eat. Promise. It's because I can't cook like you, so I don't enjoy the food as much."

"Such a flatterer." But Mom's cheeks were pink, and joy sparkled in her eyes as she sat to join us.

Dad draped an arm around the back of her chair, and his fingers played with one of her curls. Those two were always touching, always showing each other how much they loved one another. It'd been reassuring to Kieran and me, especially when so many of our friends' parents divorced. There was never a worry that would happen to ours. They inspired us for what we wanted someday. Kieran had found that in his girlfriend, Leslie, and if he'd lived to someday marry her, he would have had it.

We were silent for a few moments as we tucked into our breakfast. When I finished, I pushed my plate away, tracing my finger over the chip in the table where Kieran had tried to gouge his name when we were young. I couldn't hold it in any longer. They must have known my question was coming when I met their solemn gazes across the table. "Why are you selling?"

Mom wrung her hands but looked to my father as she said,

"Your dad is retiring at the end of the year, and the house is too big for us. We want something smaller, easier, with less work."

They embodied the image of young, hip parents. They'd fallen in love when they were eighteen and had Kieran and me a year later. Because of the way they minimized concerns and made everything look easy, I was forced to read between the lines: less stress, minimal yard work. "That makes sense. Will you stay in Honolulu?"

"Yes," Dad answered. "We're buying a condo from a friend at a steal of a price."

I furrowed my brows but didn't press for information. "I'll help in any way I can."

"That's wonderful, darling. We could use help with packing everything up. We're moving in three weeks."

"So soon?" I couldn't keep the surprise from my voice. "Why didn't you say anything?"

"We were going to call and let you know this week," Dad explained. "But you're here now."

While my parents chatted about the neighbors and how their week was going, I wrestled with the coming change while making the appropriate nods and comments. I wasn't paying close attention. My mind whirled with the looming loss of our childhood home, a place where I felt Kieran's presence most deeply.

After I helped Mom clear the table, I wandered into my room, where they said there were empty boxes. They didn't say it, but I knew it would be the same situation in Kieran's room. We'd left it mostly untouched after he died. None of us could bring ourselves to get rid of anything.

That was where I would start.

It would be hard for me and devastating for them. I didn't want them to have to carry that burden, especially after Dad's surgery. I couldn't lose them too.

I stepped into Kieran's room, and it felt as if he was there with me. I could hear him laughing and giving my hair a slight tug while he tried to convince me to go to the beach with his friends, to let loose for a change. He was gone, but there was so much life in the room. Kieran had been jammed full of it.

I walked the perimeter of his room. The lack of clothes he'd always left all over every inch of the space and the made bed were the only things that seemed unnatural. I ran my hand across his dark-gray bedspread and fought the urge to curl on it and hug the pillow to my chest. I swiped at a tear. *God, Kieran, I miss you.*

"You, too, Little K."

With a sigh, I ignored his voice in my head and got to work, sorting through his clothes in the closet, making two piles: one to donate and one to throw out. I checked all the pockets just in case there was anything secreted away. It took less time than I would have thought, probably because I was moving on autopilot.

As I moved onto Kieran's shelves and desk cluttered with memorabilia, I couldn't help but wonder who was selling our parents the condo. I needed to find out to make sure it was a good investment and that they would be safe.

But that was for later. My goal was to get through as much of my brother's stuff as I could, because I didn't know when I would be able to come back here.

His football trophies, awards, and team pictures went in another box, along with his high school yearbooks. Then there was the scholarship award and letter of admission for the university he never got to attend. Tears leaked from my eyes, and I swiped them away, taking some calming breaths. My parents wouldn't want to get rid of any of it. My hands shook from the stolen dreams and years, the promise of Kieran's potential snuffed too soon as I closed the box and wrote on the side what the contents were.

After a few moments of struggle where I almost broke down,

I got a good portion of his awards packed before facing his desk. I knew I wouldn't get through everything there, but I could go through at least one of the drawers. A squeak sounded as I pulled the right middle drawer open. It was heavy and filled to the top with a mix of pictures, a small wooden box that revealed more photos when I opened the lid, and papers. Kieran wasn't very organized. I took out the box, wanting to look through that first, as it looked like something he would have stored his most treasured pictures in. I smiled at a memory that invaded my mind from when we were younger. I'd stopped by his room late one night during my freshman year, his junior.

"God, Kier, your room is like a garbage dump. I can't even see the floor under your clothes."

He'd laughed, seated at his desk, and leaned over, yanking me inside with one of his huge hands. "Good thing I have you and Mom."

"You'd be lost without us." I'd kicked aside a pair of shorts and leaned against him as he scrolled through a paper he was working on for English.

"I'm sending this to you." He winked at me. "Can you do your editing thing?"

"Sure." Kieran always helped me with math, and I fixed all his papers. It didn't matter that we were two years apart. I was in advanced English classes, and he was in accelerated math.

I was yanked from the past when the sound of his voice filled my head as if he were standing in the room with me. "So you got the job of cleaning up after me. It's sort of like old times, isn't it?"

I swiped at the tears before they fell. My mind said Kieran wasn't there, but he sounded real, and when I turned and looked at the space where his voice was coming from, there was no way I could convince myself otherwise.

My mammoth-sized brother leaned against the opposite wall, adjacent to the room's only window.

I went with it because I needed it. "Someone's got to. I don't know how Leslie put up with you."

He threw his head back and laughed, warming my soul. When his gaze landed on me again, he tilted his head to the side. "What's that?"

My hand jerked, and I dropped the pictures on his desk, scattering them over the makeshift treasure box he'd stashed them in. Kieran pushed away from the wall and closed the distance between us. Bracing himself on the desk, he leaned over me, a lock of his black hair falling over his forehead. I tucked mine behind my ears. Our appearances were similar in so many ways, but he was dark to my light and two years older.

When he tapped the picture that'd flown out of the pile and to my right, I dropped my attention to it. In it, a bunch of his friends were congregated in our driveway.

"I remember that day." He knocked the knuckle of his index finger against the graphite-gray car in the driveway they'd stood around. "Mateo had just gotten this car. I think that was the day Vivian sunk her claws into him."

Ugh, cheerleaders. "They were always hanging around you."

He tweaked my nose. "You never were a fan of those girls. Vivian was a parasite. But you liked Leslie."

"She was the exception." His girlfriend had been the head cheerleader, and he'd been the quarterback. Not once had she excluded me or been mean. I'd liked her a lot.

"I wonder if Mateo got what he wanted." He nudged the picture with his fingertip. "The cheer team had given all of us those shark's-tooth necklaces. It was an inside joke, but it still meant something. Did you ever find mine?"

I choked back a sob. He hadn't been wearing it when the divers pulled him out of the car, but they'd found it on the side of the road, where the accident occurred.

"Hey." He swiped at the onslaught of tears streaming down my face. "I'm here. It's okay."

"But you're not."

He knelt, so we were at eye level. "I am. Even when you can't see me, I'm with you. Cheering you on."

"The bonfire's tonight," I whispered.

There was a beat of silence before he asked, "Are you going?"

"I think so."

"Then I'll see you there."

He'd always watched out for me when I went to any of the beach parties back then. What he was saying was different—he wouldn't be there to shield me. I closed my eyes briefly, willing the tears to stop. When I opened them, he was gone.

I grappled mentally with the trick my mind had played. The likeliest scenario was that I'd missed him so much that I'd conjured his image and the conversation.

Instead of dwelling on my mental state, I grabbed a handful of papers and the box with photographs and dropped them on the top of his desk. There were a few piles I had going from the drawer: paper, pictures, and miscellaneous stuff. Once it was empty, I got to work on throwing out whatever wasn't worthy of keeping: notices from the library, hall passes, and a few other various things. The graded assignments I kept separate, along with any handwritten notes. Those I would go through with Mom. Then there were the pictures. My fingers trembled as I lifted one by the corner.

Kieran hung out with a lot of people. He was everyone's friend or idol. But there was a handful of guys he was with the most. Those were the photographs I held, the ones from the box. And there were so many of him with Leslie. I traced his handsome face, so similar to mine. While my features were more delicate, his were noteworthy and masculine. I always paled in comparison to him, but I didn't mind. I liked the shadows, while he craved attention.

We used to surf together, though, and because of him, I'd

won several competitions. Each win always made me feel connected to him. I missed him so much. He was not only my brother but my best friend.

The front door opened and closed, and the sound of my parents' voices pulled me out of my memories. I flipped through a couple of the pictures, smiling at how happy Kieran looked in the pictures with his friends. There were images of the guys around a bonfire and goofing off after a homecoming game. I let the stack fall from my hands and back into the box. Then I changed my mind and shoved them and the box in my purse. I wasn't in any shape to go through them anymore that day. I would look at them again later.

The ping of my phone gave me an excuse to step away from the desk. I would come back and finish up soon. I pulled my phone from my pocket and glanced at the screen.

Roy: *Come home, or I'll come to you.*

I shivered with the sense that I wouldn't like what he would do if he found me.

I eased out of Kieran's room's dense memories and followed the happy chatter tricking into the house from the lanai. My parents preferred open windows over air conditioning. As I left the hallway where the bedrooms were, their voices were more precise, and I recognized who the visitor was—*Jaxon*.

I closed my eyes and took a steadying breath before walking out to the porch to greet him. I wasn't in any shape to be around Jaxon, but I squared my shoulders and stepped out anyway. The smile plastered on my face felt brittle, and I doubted I'd fooled him, given his narrowed eyes.

He took up so much space and not in the way I expected. He was a couple of inches over six feet tall, with broad shoulders and an athletic body. But that wasn't what was so oppressive. It was his presence. He saturated the room, drew me in, and over-whelmed me all at once.

The experience was different than it had been with Roy. He, too, had a larger-than-life persona and took up way more space than his behemoth size. But being in his orbit wasn't a particularly good thing, not anymore. I'd learned about the ugly side of his character. And I wondered if my former coworker, Stephanie, had, too—maybe that was why she'd left. The flash drive with our company's logo surfaced in my thoughts. *Did she go in a rush as well, forgetting the memory stick?*

I made a mental note to look her up at her new job and contact her about getting the flash drive back to her. Neither of us should leave a trace of ourselves with that man.

Absently, I glanced at my parents. My dad had pulled Mom onto his lap. They were always touching, laughing. Their love was legendary. I hoped to find the same someday.

"Hello again, Kayla." Jaxon's deep voice held an intimacy that caused a full-body shiver and drew my attention to him.

I broke the intense eye contact and focused on what my parents were looking at on the table: paint samples. "Is that for here?"

"No, Jaxon stopped by with these so we can pick out what colors we want to go in the condo."

"Wait." I took a step back. "Do you mean you're moving into his condo?"

"Yep." Mom smiled. "Isn't it exciting? The moving truck is all scheduled." She nervously scanned the space inside. "I'll need to get going on packing."

"Don't worry about it. I'll help. I've got a good head start on Kieran's room, and mine will be easy, as there isn't a lot left in there."

Jaxon moved around the table and paused next to me. "Let me know when you've chosen the colors, and I'll get to work." He gave my shoulder a gentle squeeze, and I sank my teeth into my bottom lip to stifle the moan that wanted to escape. "Nice seeing you again, Kayla."

"You too," I mumbled distractedly.

When he left, I turned to my parents. "He's moving out? You guys bought his place?" I parroted my earlier question, still having difficulty believing it.

"Sure did," Dad answered. "He's moving to that island of his with his brothers. He sold the condo to us as a favor when he heard we were looking for somewhere to live during retirement."

Jaxon's place had two bedrooms. I glanced at the samples on the table. I needed somewhere to stay. "I'll be right back."

I raced out the front door then hopped a flowering shrub while flagging him down as he backed out of the driveway.

He braked then rolled down the window of the squad car. "Everything okay?"

"Yeah." Now that I had his attention, I was nervous about asking. But better to bunk with him, off Roy's radar, and keep my parents safe. "I can do the painting if I can stay there. You have a spare bedroom, right?"

The sun glinted off his mahogany hair, and the sinful grin that curved his face had me holding my breath. "Does this mean you forgive me, Kayla?" He asked in that quiet way of his, the one that made me strain to hear, searching for the deeper meaning that was surely imbedded in his words. We both knew what he meant.

There was no point in dredging up bitter memories. I wasn't quite ready, but out of necessity, I would do what I had to. I held his somber gaze with one of my own. "For now."

A speculative gleam entered his dark eyes. That right there told me I was in over my head, but it didn't matter. His place was the perfect solution.

"You're welcome to the spare bedroom. I'll be home in a couple of hours. Meet me there?"

I nodded because I was incapable of speech. He'd always made me tongue-tied, unless I was raving mad about something

Kieran had done. Nothing had changed. I still had a huge crush on the guy, despite how much he had hurt me in the past.

If only things had ended differently that night.

5

KAYLA

There was garage parking for Jaxon's condo, and I pulled into a spot. It would provide even more protection if Roy was canvassing the neighborhood, not that it was that close to my parents' house. Unless he saw me coming and going, he would never have guessed I was there. My grip tightened on the steering wheel as I sat, waiting for Jaxon. I'd texted him, telling him I was on my way. He'd told me where to park and that he would be there soon.

What am I doing? He'd been one of my brother's closest friends—one who was strictly forbidden to date me. Kieran had made that clear. And we'd tried, sort of.

The humiliation and pain of the past week's events and of what I was about to do—move into Jaxon's—hurtled me into the past, to the one place I tried never to visit. To thick grass that cushioned my feet. To the second time in a matter of days where I felt the loss of my brother too profoundly.

All I'd wanted was to see his face once more, hear his laugh, for him to be alive.

The day of the funeral played out no matter how hard I tried to block it.

My bones had felt brittle and threatened to crumble under the weight of my body as I stood with my family. The smell of earth permeated the air, and I gagged on each inhalation of the putrid odor. The priest's voice was an ice pick designed to pierce my ears and make them bleed.

I swayed on my feet. We had been trapped in misery—in hell —as we laid my brother to rest.

Friends surrounded us while my brother's lifeless body lay in a fucking box, never to open his eyes again. His laugh, his joy for life, and his stolen moments haunted me. I'd cried so much I doubted my body was capable of making any more tears.

I'd been wrong.

My cheeks were wet with them as we said our last goodbye.

The trade winds swirled around us, washing away the remnants of the grave and carrying instead the scent of ocean, spice, and a hint of coconut—Kieran was near. I knew it with my heart and soul. Even with the knowledge that he was close, I couldn't escape the sense that I would drown, that the pain from the loss of my brother would consume me until I, too, didn't exist.

But I wasn't alone in my grief.

My mother's sobs had cracked something deep inside me that I feared would never be whole again. Dad shielded her in his embrace. But nothing could protect us from the reality of Kieran's body being lowered into the ground.

The priest's gravelly voice had droned on. I heard the sound and shape of it but not the words. None would do my brother justice. None would provide the comfort my much smaller family desperately needed.

We'd formed a circle around the grave. Jaxon, his brothers, and his parents were directly across from ours. A handful of others filled a U-shape, but their faces hadn't registered through my tear-filled eyes.

I'd sucked in a stuttered breath and allowed myself one look across the way. My brother's best friend, *my lover*, stood across from me with his gaze trained on the box that held Kieran. We hadn't spoken more than two words to one another. His "I'm so sorry" about killed me. I'd staggered under the weight of his words. My dad had held me up, not Jaxon. And I felt the loss of him in that moment too.

He'd told me that he'd chosen me the night we were together, rather than going out with my brother. I couldn't help but wonder if Kieran would be alive if he'd chosen differently.

When it came down to it, Jaxon hadn't been there for me. He hadn't chosen either one of us. And that was the thought had that seared me as few others could.

Other than my parents, I had been truly alone.

With a jolt, I pulled myself from the memory. Low light and cement walls filtered back into my vision, as did my steering wheel. I was in Jaxon's garage, waiting for him to meet me so that we could go up to his condo. I took measured breaths, pushing the grief away as much as I could.

I'd hated and wanted him for so long. *How can we coexist in a condo?*

His Escalade slid into the spot next to me, and I had to concentrate on prying my white-knuckled grip from the wheel. I had to do it. There was no other choice. I wouldn't risk my parents' lives by staying with them.

It was best. I could paint while he was at work. I could read at night, holed up in my room. Jaxon might not even stay there during all the painting—he had two other brothers who both owned condos, and he could stay with them.

With that happy thought, I got out of my car and retrieved my messenger bag and suitcase. Jaxon stood next to my bumper, flipping his keys around his finger in a catch and release. His brows rose at my luggage. Shoulders squared, I raised mine in challenge. With a shake of his head, he took my suitcase from me, but I moved to the side, creating enough distance that there was no risk of touching.

The garage was dimly lit but clean. We'd parked close to the elevators. As soon as the doors opened, we stepped inside, my luggage bumping over the threshold. He pressed the number seven, and we rode together without saying a word. *Awkward.*

I'd never been to his place before, but I'd heard things about him and his brothers through my parents and a few old friends. Not that I'd asked, because that was not the case.

From the corner of my eye, I could see him watching me. All the fine hairs on my body stood at attention, and my mind and body warred. I was still so hurt and angry with him, even after all those years. But none of that mattered. In spite of it all, we had crazy sexual tension. At least, I thought, neither of us would act on any physical urges—not after how things had ended.

His hand settled on my back after he opened the door to his place, and he guided me in. The touch left me shaky, and I sped ahead so his hand fell away.

My flip-flops slapped against the foyer's marble tile. It wasn't a huge area, but it was big enough for a hallway table and a simple but elegant light. From there, I could see a wall of windows leading to the lanai. Past the sliding doors, miles of turquoise shimmered in the sunlight. He had an ocean view, and it was breathtaking.

"I stopped at the hardware store and had a key made for you." He dropped his keys and wallet in a pretty blue-and-green glass bowl him mom had probably picked out. "I'll leave it here." He placed the spare key next to his. Then he pointed at a door down the hallway and to the right. "That'll be your room. We can put your things inside, and then I'll show you the place."

The bedroom was a good size and included an attached bath that I could get used to with an oversized shower that included a rainfall head and bench seat. We deposited my stuff, then I followed him as he left the bedroom.

The hallway opened up to the main space, which consisted of the kitchen along the back wall adjacent to the entrance, with a gray-and-white quartz island that flowed into the living room. There was a big-screen TV, a dark-gray L-shaped couch, and sliding glass doors that led to a decent-sized balcony overlooking the ocean. A busy road sat between us and a three-story condo building that barely obstructed the view.

A small table sat between two patio chairs complete with ottomans along one side, and a barbeque stood at the other corner. There was a leafy plant near the railing, and I pictured mornings with coffee out there. This place was perfect, and I knew my parents would love it.

"This is beautiful." I shifted so I could see him as well as the spectacular view. "Why do you want to leave it?"

Jaxon stood with his hands in his pockets and a forlorn expression I'd rarely seen on him before. "It's an expense I don't need, and since I can't see myself working as a cop, my brothers and I were talking about starting up a business on the island my family owns."

I remembered a conversation he and I had had a long time ago. His mom's family was very wealthy, and the island's ownership had been handed down on his mom's side for generations. Jaxon and his brothers were not hurting for money.

When Kieran had come back, he couldn't stop talking about it. I'd wanted to go, but I was only in junior high then, and Jaxon looked at me more like a kid sister than anything else. It wasn't until freshman year that I'd caught him staring at me with a confused expression. It was enough to give me hope, and I found every opportunity I could for our paths to cross. That was the year that I got to go to the island. It was where we held hands for the first time. When nothing came of it, I'd been crestfallen.

Dislodging from the bittersweet memory, his comment about a business finally registered. "I thought your brothers were still in the Navy."

"Tyler is. But Xander got out not long ago. He's on his honeymoon right now, but he'll be back in a couple of weeks, and that's when I'm moving."

"Ah, okay. In three weeks, when my parents are here?"

"That's the plan."

I glanced around, not seeing the supplies I would need. "Did they pick out the paint colors?"

He motioned for me to follow him to a door off the kitchen. It was a small laundry room, and a couple of cans of paint were in the corner, along with brushes and rollers. Drop cloths were folded and stacked on top of the dryer.

"I jotted down what they want where. I'll help when I'm home, but if you can get the rooms taped off and stack any pictures on the back wall in here, or even in my closet, that would help."

"Sure." I nodded.

"I'll bring up a ladder from the storage unit in the garage in a little while. I'm going to make some dinner before I have to run back to the station for about an hour. Are you hungry?"

I shrugged. "What are you making?"

"Sandwiches. Turkey, bacon, tomato, and avocado."

"Okay, but let me help." That was good. I needed to concentrate on tasks rather than how I was in a confined space with him.

He got out a frying pan and the ingredients. As the pan heated, we layered the bread. I had a choice of provolone, Swiss, or goat cheese. I went with provolone.

"This reminds me of the time we made an entire loaf into sandwiches with everything we found in the meat and cheese drawer in your house." Jaxon chuckled. "And Kieran tried to eat four at once."

"Oh, wow, that was such a mess. He spewed them all over the place. You used mayonnaise. He always hated that."

"Yeah." Jaxon put the sandwiches in the pan. "I'd forgotten that little fact." He cooked our food then set it onto plates. We carried our meal to the couch. He clicked on the news but turned the volume way down. "I hope you don't mind. I wanted to see if there was anything further about the attack this morning."

"I don't mind." Any distraction from how close he was sitting to me was good. I picked up my food and took a bite. "You can cook! This is really good."

He finished chewing then grinned. "I've got a couple of tricks up my sleeve."

I didn't want to think about what else he did well—that was dangerous territory. We ate in silence and watched the news. I couldn't help but glance around his home. There were pictures of Kieran and him, and of his brothers hanging out on the beach. The brothers were all gorgeous, but Jaxon was the one who always caught my eye, even though Xander was the one my age. An old family picture with the three boys and their parents was next to a recent one taken of Xander with his wife on the beach. They looked happy, and with a pang to my heart, I realized how much I still wanted what it appeared he had.

"Tell me about what you've been doing these past few years."

"Not much to tell." I shrugged, setting my plate on the coffee table. "I write book reviews for the *Honolulu Star-Adviser* and *Kirkus Reviews,* and I freelance for the *New Yorker* too."

"That's a good fit. If your nose wasn't buried in a book, you always had one nearby."

"Hmm." I didn't want to comment. It wasn't anything new. He and my brother used to tease me from time to time. A couple of minutes passed as we ate in silence and watched the news.

"Are you going to the bonfire tonight?"

Pain lanced through me again, so fresh from the imagined

conversation I'd had with Kieran in his room, where we'd discussed that very topic.

Why won't Jaxon stop pushing? I lashed out. "Can we not talk about things that relate to high school? We knew each other in the past. There isn't any reason to revisit it." I knew I was over-reacting, but I could only take so many memories of Kieran in one day. I didn't think the loss of my brother would ever cease to gut me.

"I'm not going to stop, Kayla, because we never resolved what happened between us that night." His voice dropped to a deep murmur, but its impact wasn't any less for it. "We need to talk about it."

Goddammit! I whirled on the couch to face him. *This entire week is a shit show.* "We need to stay away from certain topics, or we won't be able to live together. Anything with my brother is at the top of that list."

"I can't do that, Kayla. Kieran was my best friend."

I blinked furiously, clearing my vision as much as I could. All I did lately was cry. "It's better that we don't talk about that night because not only did you fail my brother, but I did too. It's something I can't come to terms with. We were selfish."

With the pad of his finger, he swiped under my eye. I jerked away from his touch, turning to stare at the TV instead. It took a second for my brain to process what I was seeing. It was a picture of Stephanie, my coworker from the paper and Roy's ex-girlfriend.

"Oh God." I couldn't tear my focus from the TV, but I sensed Jaxon's full attention.

I was chilled to the bone at the reality of what the broadcast meant and how it could have related to me. As the gravity of the situation settled like a noose around my neck, I closed the distance between Jaxon and myself. I gripped his hand, and when he lifted his arm to make room, I pressed tightly into his side.

She'd been found dead.

6

JAXON

The need to go back to work for an hour or so tore me from Kayla's side not long after she'd learned of her coworker's murder. Once she'd insisted she was fine, I went into the office. It took less time than I thought it would. Paperwork done, I hurried to return. The bonfire was that night, and I would be there with her during the second emotional roller-coaster she'd have to ride that day.

The mere possibility of Kayla staying in my condo reanimated the vision of her I had all those years ago, lying in my arms, skin on skin. I never wanted to let her go, and I shouldn't have. We were young back then, lacking the advantage of maturity. Things would be different this time around. I would make sure of it.

As I merged into traffic on my way home, I revisited the conversation I'd had earlier with Jack Davis, a former SEAL who my brothers and I knew. He'd returned my call and had given me information that connected the dots in ways that alerted every part of me to take action.

His contacts from the CIA and FBI had come through. A small militia group mistakenly recorded as dismantled years ago were suspected to have been behind the attack broadcasted on the news this morning. They called themselves Mahrib Allah and were a mix of Iranian and Venezuelan soldiers who believed they were the hand of Allah, doing His work. Although they were a small cell, they were powerful.

Tensions were high with Iran and Venezuela teaming up. The delivery of Iranian oil tankers to the El Palito port in Venezuelan was supervised without interference, even though there were rumors that nukes and various weapons were on board then smuggled into the country for a joint attack against the US. The SEALs were sent to ferret out the weapons' location to keep diplomatic relations intact.

Over the past several months, the news and the military publications I subscribed to had been discussing captured images of an Iranian tanker at the Venezuelan port. The government had issued a threat against the US, warning us not to get involved. To avoid a war, we'd complied. But there were severe concerns.

The vendetta for this group had crossed the line when they struck on US soil. I needed to know more. Xander couldn't talk about mission-specific details, as I hadn't been part of the latest missions he'd participated in.

Distracted, I let myself into the condo. Kayla was on the couch, watching the news. With a brief hello, I continued to go over all the information I'd gleaned regarding the multiple explosions.

"Are you all right?"

Her voice snagged my attention. I shook my head. "The explosions. I've been thinking about what that means for my parents."

Kayla sat with her legs tucked under herself. I paced, having a hard time curtailing the need for action. All five of the victims' names from the explosions ran through my head. It was a small miracle there weren't more fatalities, based on where the murders occurred.

"How can I help?"

Her voice eased my mind, halting my trek around the living room. "All three men that were killed were former Navy SEALs. Two of the victims were their wives." I shared the details with her from the profiles of the victims. "There is a militia cell we suspect, but what we haven't figured out is how they're getting data on the former SEALs. It's not as if they were all struck in their homes." Then I gave voice to what worried me most. "It's the same team my dad served on."

"Oh, no." The color leached from her face. "What are you going to do?"

"I've called. My dad is aware of the threat. We don't know the details of the tracking and kill strikes surrounding the former SEALs, especially since there isn't collateral damage to others—meaning the murders are specific. The message was meant to be uncontested with the addition of misleading bodies."

"Jax, I'm so sorry. Please let me know how I can help." She twined her fingers together, wringing them in obvious worry. "Had the other SEAL families followed a routine?"

"That's the first thing we checked. The Greers were home. The Barstows' daughter was home ill with her child, and her parents were in her flower shop hours before they were due to open it. The Vincents were in their car, having left an early breakfast in central Honolulu. It's the two not at home who were the odd men out, so to speak."

"But the men all served together?" She tilted her head to the side, and I paused, momentarily distracted.

It was enough to jostle other details into focus about the case. The targeted hits went deeper, tying into a recent mission —an excursion I was aware of because I'd also participated in one to Colombia and Venezuela, where my team leader, John, had been killed. Xander and now Tyler would have been sent on similar missions, as the unrest was very real.

"They did," I said. "Same unit. Another disturbing fact is that the Greers' son was recently killed on a mission that Xander was on. The vendetta had to be based around something the former SEALs did. A mission carried out. Most likely from South America or Iran." Fingers of white-hot fear skated along my spine. My parents—all of us were at risk if they were going after SEALs. Maybe not just the ones on the retired members' team—not if Kyle and John were both killed. I didn't share that detail with Kayla. My immediate concern was my parents and the other members of the older team because their brothers had been struck down on US soil.

The pieces were connecting. My gut instinct said the two teams had to be connected to Mahrib Allah's vendetta.

"Why Iran?" Kayla leaned forward. "Does this have anything to do with the news report about the Iranian oil tanker docking at a Venezuelan harbor?"

I gave her a quick recap of my suspicion about what the tanker had carried and the threat issued from the Venezuelan president, should the Navy have gotten involved.

"But"—her eyes widened—"that means you're in danger. And your brothers."

I held her gaze and nodded.

She stilled. "Oh God, Jax." Tears misted her eyes before she blinked them away and picked up her phone. "I wonder…" With a tap of her finger, she opened her Facebook app, typed in "Susan Barstow," scrolled through her timeline, then did the same with Kathy Vincent. Then she handed me the phone.

"Both Susan and Kathy posted about what they were doing early that morning. If the militia was following the wives on social media, their movements were well documented," she said.

Everything in me hardened. I typed in mom's name. *Goddammit.* There were so many pictures of her and dad on the boat. Nothing from the past few days, luckily, but that didn't mean there wouldn't be or that they weren't already being tracked. I knew a drone could easily find them and drop a very precise bomb.

My parents were in danger. I hit redial on Dad's number. He hadn't picked up before, but I would call until he did.

"Your parents are on the boat." Kayla would have heard from her dad. "I can get the Coast Guard to warn them. I still volunteer with them. I could go too."

"I don't want you in danger. Going to the boat puts you in harm's way." I turned to the sliding glass doors and the view of the tumultuous ocean as soon as I heard Dad's groggy voice —alive.

"Dad. Delete Mom's social media. The recent explosions may be from tracking their targets' accounts." I knew he would be up to date via Navy and military articles he was on top of and the news he watched every morning and evening through a satellite feed on the boat. I recapped what Kayla and I had discussed and her discovery about the possibility of how the militia group had found their marks.

By the time we hung up, we'd formed a plan about planting false leads about where they were and what they were up to. Their location would ping from those locations with the help of Chris Shaw, a member of the Gray Ghost team, who I would also involve.

After talking with Chris, the next step was to go to the station and update Nolan. He was the lead detective, so I had to turn over details and let him run with it. My connection to the case also was a clear sign to turn the data over. But I needed a minute alone with Kayla before I left.

After I hung up, I rounded the coffee table and drew Kayla to her feet, wrapping her in my embrace. "Thank you. You may have just saved their lives."

7

KAYLA

After blotting my face dry with a towel, I stood in front of the sink and reapplied my makeup. Jaxon waited for me in the other room. He'd insisted we go to the bonfire together after he held me as the newscaster reported the details, or lack thereof, regarding Stephanie's death, while I'd fallen apart in his arms.

She was found along the harbor, near a fish processing warehouse and down the road from some local clubs. Other than that, nothing else was known.

Stephanie and I had barely known each other, but we had worked at the same newspaper, exchanged pleasantries, and dated the same guy—which was alarming.

We'd crossed a line from distant to something more. When Jaxon confided about his fears over the explosions and included me in searching for a solution, we shifted away from the bitterness I'd harbored. It was a lot to process.

I was getting ready for the bonfire and taking my time while Jaxon waited for me. There wasn't much I could do about my swollen eyes. Eye drops took care of the redness, and foundation hid the remnants of the faded yellow-green bruising along my cheek and neck, which he'd stared at too long with a hard, unreadable expression.

My eyeliner pencil slipped from my fingers and clattered in the sink. Shit. I hunched over the counter, hanging my head. I was confused. In Jaxon's arms, everything felt right. But nothing good had ever come from the two of us being together, no matter how much I wanted things to be different.

The one and only time we had been together, my brother died. And if I gave in again, I feared that Jaxon would die.

What I was doing wasn't fair to him. I was putting him in harm's way, and I wanted to keep my problems all to myself, even though that was selfish. And from the way he looked at me, I knew I had to confess everything soon but not that night. I couldn't take much more.

One last check in the mirror to make sure everything was covered that needed to be, and I shoved away from the sink then opened the door. I had on an old pair of jean shorts, a stretchy blue-gray V-neck, and an oatmeal cardigan because I couldn't shake the chill after learning about Steph.

Jaxon had insisted on going together after I fell apart, and I was more than okay with it. When I entered the living room, he leaned against the frame of the open sliding glass doors, letting the outside in. Without the TV on, the sound of the waves filled the space. It was peaceful and made me long for simpler times. Maybe that was what I could find now that I was single again.

He turned at my approach, his gaze heating as he gave me a slow perusal from head to toe, closing the distance between us. When he slipped his hand in mine and pressed a kiss to the top of my head, I soaked up the warmth of his touch, promising myself that he was a friend, not an enemy or a lover, and I could exist in the simple gesture.

The night promised to be hard enough as it was. The annual bonfire for Kieran was at a secluded beach that only island natives frequented. Its access was off the beaten path. We got into Jaxon's Escalade and drove in silence.

It didn't take too long until we were pulling through dense vegetation, bumping along the hidden dirt-and-sand road that opened up to a small clearing at the edge of the beach. Cars crowded the small opening and lined the makeshift road. To park, we had to back up, maneuvering between two trees off the worn trail.

Orange flames licked the dark sky, reflecting off the closest clouds. Tiki torches were set up, lining the beach. It was inviting, something Kieran would have loved. I rubbed a hand over my aching heart as Jaxon and I walked to join everyone.

He squeezed my hand. "Want anything to drink?"

"Definitely."

I barely heard his "be right back" before a group of three women approached him. My body heated, and I recognized the emotion for what it was—jealousy. They had a chance with him. I never had.

Tearing my gaze from the four of them, I scanned the people there. I knew a majority of them. Turning my back to the little scene, I perused the chair groupings scattered around, including those farther from the fire. I made my way to a small cluster on the outskirts, where I was more comfortable. Jaxon knew where to find me.

A woman stood from one of the areas that I was walking toward. She took a few steps as she waved at some other people and was about to join them when she spotted me. She changed directions to intercept me.

"Kayla." Vivi reached out and clasped my hands, a wide smile stretching her pretty face. From what I could tell from the firelight, she had already had a few beers. But the girl I'd known in the past had changed. Her bright eyes sparkled before she pulled me in for a hug. "I'm so glad you came tonight. We've all missed you."

I returned her squeeze and smiled when she pulled back. "Thanks, Vivi."

"I'll catch up with you later. I need to grab another drink." She squeezed me once more then went in the direction of a cooler. *Huh, the jealous cheerleader in the past isn't there anymore.* Marriage to Mateo must have mellowed her. She seemed happy, which was good. He was a great guy and deserved to be married to this new, improved version, not the one I'd known back then.

With Vivi waylaid on her way back by a couple of people, I spotted a rather large man sprawled in one of the chairs I'd been heading for. When he lifted his hand in a wave, I grinned and closed the distance.

"Hey, Mateo." I dropped into one of the beach chairs. "How's it going?"

"Good, Little K."

I turned, shielding my features so he wouldn't see the grimace. The football players used to call me "Little K" because my brother and I shared the same first letter in our names. Sometimes, even Kieran had called me that. It was a bitter-sweet memory, and I suspected I would have to deal with a lot of that at the bonfire. But I was there, and it was time to heal some of the old wounds, even if I would never stop missing him.

"So you and Vivi?" I'd heard about the wedding in their freshman year of college. Just the thought of where they were in life and all they'd experienced growing up together hit home. I hadn't shared my past with Roy, only my present, and I'd thought there was a possibility of a future too.

"Yeah," He took a long pull from his beer then drew me back to the conversation. "We got married in college."

"Kids?"

"Nah. She never wanted to be a mom. But what about you? It's been forever."

Might as well dive in deep. "I'm still working for the paper. But

I thought it was time I came home and went to one of Kieran's bonfires."

Mateo huffed out a heavy sigh with something like deep-set grief carving lines around his usually smiling mouth. "If Kieran were here, there's so much I'd want to say to him. But he was never about regrets or what-ifs, ya know?" He shook his head, tipping his beer back for another drink. "It's good that you came. He would have liked that."

I kicked my legs out and crossed my ankles just as Jaxon appeared with a beer. "Thanks," I murmured then downed half the contents. He set another in the cupholder in the armrest. That was one thing about Jaxon I adored—even though he was quiet, he didn't miss anything. And if I were to survive the night, I would need a lot of alcohol to do it.

"Jaxon." Mateo grinned. "I heard you're a cop."

"Temporarily," Jaxon said. "How's the auto shop?"

"It's a job." He flashed another easygoing grin. "Being a mechanic has its headaches, but with my bum shoulder, it beats doing grunt work."

"I heard about that." His injury had been a career-ending one. I finished off the rest of my drink then handed the empty to Jax. "That had to be hard. You wanted to go into the NFL, right?"

"Mm-hmm," Mateo agreed. "Harder for Vivi, I think. But I'm good with our lot in life. You been surfin' lately, Little K?"

"Here and there. I need to get back out and train for Pipe."

"Hells yeah. We'll come to cheer you on. You still surfin', Jax?" Mateo asked, and they fell into a discussion about memorable waves and football while I zoned out, watching the people and catching snippets of their conversations.

Some were hard to listen to because they talked about memories they had with my brother, but it was also good to know he was alive to them, too, if only in their hearts. An easy beachy vibe encompassed all of us as the soft strains of an acoustic guitar shifted the atmosphere from partying to nostalgia.

I choked on my beer, enduring Jax's thump on my back as Mitch sang Kieran's favorite song, which I knew they did every year. Tears flowed down my cheeks, and Jax pulled me into his lap. I stayed there, cradled in his embrace, warm and safe while Mitch's deep, melodic voice danced over the waves and conjured all the times my brother used to break out into song on starry nights while we partied around the bonfire. God, I missed him.

8

JAXON

The night air had cooled significantly, and so far away from the fire, Kayla shivered. I lifted her into my arms to share body heat without protest. Mateo droned on about restoration work on an older car. Vivi had rejoined him, taking Kayla's seat. I had been done with the scene not long after it began. After talking with the few people I'd come to see, I only waited for Kayla to say the word, and we would head out.

She curled against me, resting her head on my chest, and I inhaled the scent of her. She didn't know it, but she was my world—or the one I wanted. Talking with those two was never close to ranking high on my list of things to do, especially when I had Kayla all to myself without the natural barriers she continuously erected in my presence.

I made my excuses, left, and carried her to the car. She stirred once when I got her into the passenger seat and buckled her in but fell back to sleep immediately afterwards.

Stars dotted the sky, and the moon vied for attention. I maneuvered us out of the tight self-made parking place between two palm trees, grateful that a coconut hadn't fallen and dented my car.

There had been a lot of people at the bonfire for Kieran, and with Kayla present, the secret I held burned in my gut. Eventually, it would come out. Secrets always did. What worried me most was how she would take the news and if I would lose her for good.

Before long, I'd pulled into my parking space in the condo's garage. Shutting the car off, I turned to look at Kayla, sleeping soundlessly. She was so at peace in that moment, but I knew her truth—or a part of it. She was broken. More than anything, I wanted to help her pick the pieces back up and glue them together, chasing the sorrow she carried around and making her stronger.

I got out, rounded the car, and carefully lifted her into my arms. She stirred once with a soft "what?" before passing out again. We rode the elevator to my floor, and I manipulated the lock open so we could enter. Kicking my shoes off, I went straight to my bedroom, where I'd wanted her from the moment she'd stepped inside my home.

Once she was on the bed, I took her sandals off and pulled the covers over her. I wanted to make her more comfortable by shimmying her out of her little shorts and her bra at least, but I didn't have that right. Again, she stirred, blinking bleary eyes at mine. Her mouth formed a silent question.

"Shh, we're home. Get some sleep." I brushed a kiss across her forehead. Her eyelids fluttered, and her long lashes rested against her cheeks before she drifted off.

After I got ready for bed, I crawled under the covers on the opposite side then pulled her close. It was the only privilege with her I could take, at least for the time being. I hoped things would change. Her wanting to stay here and do the painting for her parents gave me several days to try to get past her barriers and help her heal from the loss of her brother, which she'd never come to terms with.

Throughout the years, I'd wrestled with the possibility of

her, and I had a chance I would not pass up. She didn't realize it, but she'd always been mine, and I hers.

I ran my fingers through her hair, and she snuggled fully against my side, her head resting on my shoulder. I'd never felt so complete.

Again, the promise I made to Kieran would be broken, because I had to have her in my life. I had loved her forever, and it was only deepening.

Having her with me was a second chance. Not only that, but I suspected she needed my help. Those marks on her neck were the size and general layout of a handprint. I'd seen that before, and it enraged me that someone could have hurt Kayla.

I'd given her the day to keep her secrets and her past to herself. I glanced at the clock and noted it we were already into the early morning hours. At full light, she would tell me what happened and who the danger was. Because this woman was the one I wanted to keep for all of my tomorrows. Making sure she was safe, happy, and loved was my highest priority.

9

KAYLA

Tiny drums pounded inside my head, and my mouth tasted like cotton. I was burning up on one side of my body. Before I pried open my sandpaper eyelids, I tried to piece together what had happened. The last thing I remembered was talking to Mateo and Jaxon handing me one beer after another. It got a little fuzzy after that.

No, I remembered waking while in Jax's car and again when we came back to the condo. But nothing after that. I could feel sweat beading along my hairline and my cheek wet with drool. I shifted to turn on my other side and find a dry spot on the hard pillow when a band tightened around my back, holding me in place. A wave of horror hit me, and I forced my eyes open. I wasn't lying on a pillow but sprawled on top of Jaxon—and I was drooling on him!

In my head, the marching band increased to an alarming tempo with my utter embarrassment and excessive alcohol consumption. I took hasty inventory and almost whimpered with relief over the small miracle that I was fully clothed. He was hard enough to resist when I was sober. With slow movements, hoping not to wake him, I tried to slip from his arms.

"Where are you going?" His gruff, sleepy voice sent a wave of desire through me despite my hangover.

I managed to croak, "Bathroom," and as soon as his arm loosened, I fled to the bathroom to brush my teeth and splash water on my face. Arms braced on the sink, I took a breath then lifted my gaze to the mirror, cringing at my chalky complexion. A shudder ran through me, and I fought against the saliva pooling in my mouth. Sweat broke out along my hairline for the second time. With slow, measured breaths between frantic swallowing, I managed to survive the moment rather than hugging the toilet and purging my bad decisions from the night before.

After rinsing my face and mouth again, I left the bathroom and faltered. Jaxon was still in bed. The sheet stopped just below his belly button, and my eyes traveled from that spot, across chiseled abs, to his strong, broad shoulders and sexy-as-hell biceps, and finally ending on his sinfully gorgeous face. With his eyes closed, I allowed myself this moment. He was so handsome, and I'd wanted him for as long as I could remember. He and Kieran had been best friends, and on occasion, I used to tag along with them. It was always at the beach. Once there, we surfed together. Included in their circle, I would bask in the attention.

I'd always had a crush on Jaxon. He had a quiet strength about him. But when he did talk, I used to lean forward to catch every word. And when he looked at me, focusing all that intensity on my way, I was lost.

Another wave of longing swept over me.

When he grinned, my entire world brightened. If Kieran had let me, I would have followed them everywhere just for the possibility of Jaxon seeing me for more than his best friend's little sister.

Then, one day, he had.

I remembered our date like it was yesterday and let myself fall back in time to experience it again.

I'd wiped damp palms on my blue-silk wrap dress as Jaxon and I sat on a balcony table at La Mer. When he'd suggested it as our first date, I'd melted even more. Well-known, the fine-dining establishment served French cuisine with tropical ingredients. I hadn't been entirely sure about that part, but we'd both found something to order, and the food had lived up to its reputation.

There was plenty for us to talk about, and we chatted for the two hours we'd dined together. And on the lulls, we didn't need to fill the silence with constant chatter—we had our own way of communicating. It was in the touch of his hand on my arm, the way his mesmerizing brown eyes would make me feel as if I was the only woman he'd ever seen. In his presence, the beautiful view paled in comparison. My heart soared when he made me the sole recipient of the wicked grin that curved his too-kissable mouth, the one I planned to experience firsthand when he took me home.

I'd declined dessert, and instead, we enjoyed the ocean view for a few more minutes until the check came. The scrape of his chair raised goosebumps along my exposed skin as he moved closer to me. When his arm draped across my shoulders, I leaned into his warmth.

"This was a great first date." I smiled at him then confessed my secret. "I didn't think you'd ever ask me out."

His fingers trailed up and down my bare arm. "I've wanted to for a year."

Better late than never. "I'm glad you did." Heat sizzled between us, and I found it hard to breathe evenly. He was too close, and he affected me on so many levels. We'd known each other almost all my life, and I'd wanted him for about half of it.

Lights twinkled at the front of the beach, and salt hung heavily in the air as we listened to the rhythmic roll of the waves breaking along the shore. It was spellbinding and romantic. Jaxon could have taken me to a picnic on the beach with sandwiches, and I'd have had the same experience. I didn't need fancy, but it was sweet that he wanted to take me out.

"I promise I'll break the news to Kieran about us dating. He's preoccupied with Leslie and college this fall. I'm sure he'll be happy about it. I was supposed to go somewhere with him tonight, but I'll see him tomorrow."

A party? I didn't want to ask. It was enough that he'd chosen to spend the evening with me instead. But my brother might not have seen it the same way. "Maybe, but it's my life. I get to make the decisions about who I date." I scowled and inched away, annoyed by how he and my brother liked to interfere in my love life or lack thereof.

"You decided to go out with me tonight. And I'm hoping you will again."

I tilted my head so that I could meet his gaze. "Is this more than a one-time thing?"

With his free hand, he cupped the side of my face, his thumb caressing back and forth, sending a buzz of electricity in its wake. He bent so that our lips were millimeters apart, pausing to give me a chance to pull away. But that was not what I wanted, and I closed the separation.

He took control, brushing his lips across mine, teasing. Heat spiraled from the touch, and desire consumed me. I pressed my hands to his chest. His rapidly beating heart beneath my fingertips matched my thundering pulse.

"Kayla," he whispered, and my heart fluttered.

The naked need in his voice was my undoing. With an irresistible sweep of his tongue, he deepened the short kiss. When he pulled back, our breath mingled.

"Let's go." I hadn't recognized my lust-filled voice. But I'd known I wanted him to come home with me. I'd given him my first kiss, and I'd wanted him to be all my firsts.

I jolted from the memory and back to reality. We would never happen again. There were too many things between us. I hardened myself as much as possible and took a step to escape to the kitchen when he opened his eyes.

One brow lifted, and that sexy smirk he sometimes wore pulled his lips into a crooked grin. "Going somewhere?"

"Coffee," I managed to get out.

His abs flexed, and I groaned at the sight. A quiet chuckle was his response, and my face flamed. The sheets were flung back, and I went weak in the knees. He wore only tight black boxer briefs. Everything was on display, and I drank him in from a safe distance. He bent and retrieved his jeans, shoved his legs into them, then turned that intense gaze my way.

I was in big trouble.

"Come on." He grabbed my hand and threaded our fingers together, pulling me from his bedroom and into the kitchen.

When he let go to start the coffee, I climbed onto a barstool. *What is going on?* He acted as though we'd picked up where he left off when I was in high school. *Did something happen last night?*

Still processing that we'd slept in the same bed and in his bedroom, I stayed silent. The aroma of coffee saturated the air, and when he slid a mug in front of me, already doctored with cream, I took a fortifying sip. "Thank you."

"I'll make you an omelet. Then I have to go into work." He got the pan heated and started beating the eggs. "Are you feeling okay?"

After several sips of my coffee, I was returning to a somewhat functional state. "I'm fine. Thanks for bringing me home."

He put the wonderful-smelling food onto two plates and set mine in front of me, along with silverware.

I needed normalcy and grasped the first thing that came to my mind. "I'll get going on prepping for painting today."

"That's not going to work, Kayla."

With a forkful of food halfway to my mouth, I paused. "What?"

He leaned down on folded arms, his gaze boring into mine. "You can't avoid me forever. We can talk about painting, but there are more important things to discuss. I'll be back at lunch, and we're going to have a real conversation."

From Roy, I would have been shaking with a full-fledged panic attack coming on, but I'd never had anything to fear from Jaxon. I would stay at his place—and needed to until I was sure Roy wouldn't follow me to my parents'. Resigned, I agreed.

We finished our food, and after the dishes were in the dishwasher, he rounded the island and pulled me to my feet. Wrapping me in a hug, he kissed the top of my head. "Are you sure you're feeling okay?"

I nodded against him, not trusting my voice.

"I'm going to grab a fast shower and head out, but I'll be back around lunchtime."

With another kiss to the top of my head, he extracted himself from our hug. I felt a profound loss—those two kisses made me feel like he was saying goodbye to his best friend's little sister.

Confusion warred with desire, and I gasped from the overwhelming mix of emotions in the aftermath of leaving the embrace that I didn't want him to think of in that way. The ill feelings I'd harbored toward him didn't matter in the wake of that realization. We'd had one night together where we were more, and I wanted all of him—damn the consequences.

KAYLA

Jaxon had left for work, and I moved slowly through the morning hours, feeling better but still recovering from my drinking binge the night before. After pouring a second cup of coffee, I went out on the balcony to enjoy some fresh air and the absence of the mariachi band thundering in my head. I'd only had three or four beers—I was such a lightweight.

The rhythmic rise and fall of the waves in the distance soothed me even more, even though I had missed the spectacular colors of the sunrise. The sun had climbed higher. It would have been nice to enjoy a cup of coffee and watch the new day begin with the sun painting the sky. *Maybe tomorrow.*

I planned to spend half an hour relaxing before getting to work on taping the ceilings and trim so I could start cutting before using the roller to paint the rooms. Jaxon had left me an organized list of what colors would go where. It wouldn't take too long. Getting the condo ready for my parents to move in, helping them pack, and finishing my work for the paper meant it would be a busy week. I suddenly remembered that I wanted to look through the pictures I'd swiped from Kieran's room. I wanted to go through them by myself, without Mom or Dad walking in.

I got my purse from where Jaxon must have left it on the hall table then settled back on the cushioned chair, propped my feet on the ottoman, and enjoyed the cool morning air as I pulled a stack of photos from the box he'd kept them in. As I took them out, I felt something at the bottom. I set the pictures on the side table so I could see.

It was the shark's-tooth necklace that the cheerleaders had given each of the football players. *Had Mom or Dad put it in here?* Kieran used to joke that it was a noose around some of their necks when he'd learned that Vivi was the one who'd organized it. His girlfriend, Leslie, had already given him a dark-gray bead-and-silver necklace, similar to what most surfers had, that he wore instead.

I had flipped through a couple of pictures before Kieran entered my peripheral vision. I set them down, barely glancing at the image I'd paused on last time. My heart sped up, pounding painfully in my chest. I was afraid to turn my head, worried he would disappear. But even from a side view, my sight wasn't normal. It was 360 degrees, almost surreal. Then he spoke, and I gave in with tear-filled eyes to drink in the sight of my brother with the vision I was more comfortable with.

"What are you doing?" The weight of his question laded Kieran's usual carefree voice.

Is he referring to hanging out with Jaxon? I once overheard a conversation between the two of them, where Kieran forbade him to look at me as anything but a little sister. I'd cried for hours before determination set in. It was my life. "You mean being here, in Jaxon's home?"

"No." Kieran's features, so like mine, were set in tense lines, his lips pressed tightly together. "You're where you should be."

I tilted my head, confused. "I don't understand, then."

He took a step closer and reached out. I closed my eyes,

pretending I could feel his hand holding mine. "I mean about Roy—he's coming for you, Little K, and you've got to be ready. Don't have your head in the sand as I did."

My eyelids popped open, but Kieran had vanished. *Don't go.* I pulled my knees to my chest and stared at the spot where he'd stood. It was never enough time, and I missed him desperately. The first year, it had been hard to go on without him. We had always been close.

My phone rang inside my purse. My fingers struggled to get the zipper open. I finally did. Phone in hand, fear washed over me as I huddled in the safety of Jaxon's house. Roy's name lit up the screen like a bad omen. I let it go to voicemail. Not even a minute later, a threatening text came through. I couldn't go anywhere without worrying about him finding me.

Minutes turned into half an hour as I sat on the balcony. I never should have moved into Roy's place, but he'd insisted, and at the time, I'd thought it was sweet. The longer we were together, the more aggressive and jealous he had become. Then there were all those instances where I would catch him checking out other women, getting texts late at night. Doubt had set in, and I'd questioned him. Huge mistake. I'd planned to move out, but he paid more attention to me, and for a while, things were good again—until they weren't.

I wondered if Stephanie went through the same thing, if she'd left, too, and he'd come for her. If that was the case, and I was almost positive it was, he would come for me too. I couldn't keep it from Jaxon any longer. It wasn't fair, and I needed his help.

1 1

JAXON

The morning passed in agonizing slowness. As soon as I was able to take lunch, I did. When I opened the door to my condo, faint strands of "All I Want" by Kodaline drifted from the living room. I dropped my keys into the bowl on the hallway table and grinned at the sight that greeted me.

Kayla was on the ladder, applying a strip of painter's tape, toned and sexy in a tiny pair of shorts and a stretchy top. I wanted to run my hands along the insides of her legs but didn't want to freak her out.

I liked seeing her in my home, was aware of what a gift it was, and would use the time to bridge the cavernous gap between us.

At least the anger she wore as armor had dissipated. She'd hated me, blamed me for so many years. Guilt gnawed at me because of Kieran's secret—the one that could sever the possibility of Kayla and me. I shook the thought away, determined to foster the connection we had into the unbreakable bond we should have had.

Unable to resist her any longer, I rounded the couch and

61

curled my hands around her small hips so she wouldn't fall if I startled her. "You got a lot done."

She looked over her shoulder, and I caught a flash of worry or panic clouding her eyes before she masked it with a smile. "The other rooms are taped. And"—she lifted to her toes and tore the tape before securing the end in the corner—"the bathroom painting is finished."

I lifted her from the ladder and set her on the ground. She turned in my arms then sidestepped, avoiding the ladder. I reluctantly let her put space between us. The scent of tomato sauce and melting cheese cut through the smell of freshly painted walls, and I gave her the out she seemed to need. "You made something?"

"I did!" her smile widened, and she set the tape on one of the ladder stairs. "Chicken parmesan is in the over. It'll be ready in five minutes. I've got a salad in the fridge."

"Did you go shopping?"

"I ran down to the store at the end of the block and picked up a few things, but you had most of it here." She pulled a glass bowl from the fridge and put it on the island. "Help yourself."

Two places were already set, and I dished salad into both bowls. She spooned potato hash with chopped bacon onto our plates then, when the timer went off, got the chicken Parmesan out. My mouth watered. I hadn't realized how hungry I was.

She settled on the barstool beside me, and I leaned close to whisper, "This is you stalling so we don't talk about last night, isn't it?"

The corners of her lips twitched, but she leveled me with that innocent look she'd perfected when we were young and she'd done something she wasn't supposed to. Like when she hid in the back seat of Kieran's car the one time we weren't going to take her surfing with us because we were meeting some girls.

"I don't know what you're talking about," she deadpanned. "I made lunch because I thought you'd have to get back to the station soon."

"I'm only working half days, sweetheart. Today is an exception." I gave her long hair a gentle tug. She pulled back, and we dug into our food. We ate in silence for a few minutes.

"Wow, this is amazing," I said. "Who knew you would learn to cook?"

"Please. I made stuff for you and Kieran all the time."

Finishing the last bite of my chicken, I turned to her. "Yeah, you did. But it was reluctantly and only when Kieran would beg you to make one of your famous grilled-cheese-and-tomato sandwiches."

"I've gotten better and make several different paninis now." A bittersweet look crossed her face. "He would have loved them."

"I'm sure." I waited for a beat. "I'll love them. Anything you do interests me."

She swiveled in her chair, crossing one long leg over the other, and I fought the urge to run my hand along her thigh and pull her to sit with me. I wanted her closer, but we had to talk, and everything about her was distracting.

"I'll clean this up, and we can talk on the couch." I stood, but she put her hand in mine, stopping me from picking up the plates.

"I'll take care of it later." She wrung her hands and went to the couch. "Let's talk before you have to go back."

We got settled with a few inches separating us—probably for the best, so we could hash through as much as time would allow. I got right to the point. "There were moments we had together in the past that I've never been able to forget, Kayla. All of them left a lasting impression. The times we surfed, the fleeting touches. I was always aware of you, and I fought it for as long as I could."

"Because Kieran told you he'd come after you if you ever looked at me as anything other than a kid sister?"

She was always sneaky. "You heard that, huh?"

"Yeah." She worried her bottom lip. "At first, I wondered why I wasn't getting asked out on dates when all my friends were. I was so mad at both of you." Her eyes narrowed. "Don't even try to pretend you weren't a part of Kieran threatening any boy who showed the slightest interest in me."

"Wasn't going to." What she didn't know was that I wasn't doing it for the same reason her brother was. I'd always been aware of her. We'd had a connection from the moment we met, just as I had with Kieran, but the one I had with her developed into much more. As she grew, so did my feelings for her. She went from my best friend's little sister to a girl I wanted so badly it hurt. But she was two years younger and Kieran's sister. Some boundaries couldn't be crossed—until those very lines of demarcation had to be breached.

"Then you noticed me." She peered at me from beneath her lashes. "That night with you was everything I'd hoped for and wanted. Until it wasn't."

I clasped her hand in mine. "The timing wasn't right. Keep the two separate because, Kayla, you're all I ever wanted. I've never stopped thinking about you."

The moment I said that I regretted the pain it'd caused her. Because she had to have been thinking about what happened during our stolen night—her brother's death. I wanted a little time with her before telling her some of what I knew, the part I'd been sworn to secrecy over.

Tears welled then spilled down her cheeks, and I pulled her into my arms while she cried, probably for the time we'd lost. Running my hand up and down her back, I waited for her to calm. It didn't take long. When she eased back, I wiped the wetness from her face with the pads of my thumbs. Holding her wasn't enough. I needed all of her.

I cupped the back of her neck and drew her to me. When we were an inch apart and her breath intermingled with mine, I closed the distance, brushing my lips across hers in a slow caress, giving her every opportunity to pull back if she wanted. When she didn't, I applied a little more pressure, keeping a tight hold on my desire. She was so soft. Her lips parted, and I deepened the kiss, exploring and tasting. Our tongues tangled together, and a shot of overwhelming need threatened the tenuous grasp I had on my control. I didn't have all the time I wanted and forced myself to slow the kiss. When we broke apart, I rested my forehead against hers, shaken by how much I wanted her. "Give what we could have another chance, Kayla."

A tremor ran through her body before she whispered, "Yes."

Kayla

As THE WORD passed my lips, the one that told Jaxon I was all in, that I wanted to give a relationship between us another try, my mind catapulted to the night we'd shared together. Held in his arms, my lips swollen from his kiss, I succumbed to what we once had, in exquisite anticipation of what we would again.

The evening of our very first date, when I was still in high school and Jaxon had just graduated, we'd left dinner and gone to my house. The house was dark when I opened the front door, leading Jaxon inside by our clasped hands. My parents were out with friends, and Kieran was wherever he was—no one was home.

We toed off our shoes, I locked the door, and then I pulled him toward my bedroom. Electricity sizzled between us. My heart beat so fiercely that it was difficult to hear the silence around us. *Is he nervous too?*

I wanted it. Him. It didn't matter that our dating was new.

He'd been my forever crush. Things between us had changed. He was my reality, my future.

In the fall, change would come again, but we would manage. I did not doubt our destiny—he was my everything. And as we'd talked during dinner and on the way home, I knew I was his too.

The click of the door sounded as he shut it behind him then linked both our hands. We stood together in the twilight of my room, on the edge of a precipice. "Are you sure about this, Kayla?" His thick dark hair fell across his forehead as he angled down to meet my gaze.

I nodded. "Yes. Very much."

"You're so beautiful," he murmured as he released my hands, closed the distance, and threaded his fingers through my long, wavy hair. When he tilted my head, our gazes met, and I whimpered at the naked desire swimming in his dilated pupils.

I spanned my fingers across his chest, the staccato beat of his heart reassuring me that I wasn't the only one who was on the edge of losing control.

I had wanted him for so long. He brushed his lips against mine in a soft caress that had me melting. I deftly unbuttoned his shirt, wanting to feel the ridges and muscles flex beneath my touch as I inhaled his intoxicating scent.

He nipped and teased my lips while we struggled to free him from his shirt. When it was off, he went to kiss me again, but I held out my hand. "Wait. I want to see all of you. To go slow." I'd imagined the two of us together more times than I could count. I wanted to savor every touch, memorize every expression, and enjoy being with him.

With a nod, he removed all but his black boxer-briefs. It wasn't as if I hadn't seen him in board shorts countless times, but the sight of him in the tight black underwear left little to the imagination. I inched closer, exploring the hard ridges and tightly corded muscles first with my eyes then my hands. He drew me to him. Our bodies fit together as if we were made for each other. His fingers skimmed across my silk-clad back as I did the same to his naked one.

All it had taken was one touch, and I was his.

"We don't have to do anything you don't want to," he murmured in my ear, and I shivered. "You're in control with how much or little we do. Even if you want to stop now."

He eased me back, and we faced each other. I realized again how much I didn't want to hold back. "I want to experience everything with you." I pinched the tie holding half of my wrap dress together at the front side of my waist.

"Wait." Jaxon's warm hand stilled mine. "Let me."

His deep voice elicited a full-body shiver. I surrendered completely. My hand fell away, giving him access. A burning intent rearranged his features from handsome to sin worthy. He worked the knot loose then undid the small snap that secured the other side. I trembled with desire at his feather-light touch as he eased the gaping silk from my shoulders so that it pooled at my feet. I stood before him in a matching black lace bra and thong.

He lifted me into his arms and lay me on the bed, on top of my dusty-pink comforter. We locked eyes in silent understanding, and I grinned at the promise of the inferno to come.

He made quick work of the rest of our clothes then lay beside me and pulled me into his arms. We fit together, my softness nestled against his hardness. Whiskers shadowed his strong jaw, tickling my skin as he rained kisses along my neck, to my shoulders, and across the swell of my breasts. I glided my fingers through his hair, tugging him back to my lips, needing more of him.

Slowly, his hands trailed up the inside of my thigh as he took my lips in a scorching kiss. My core heated in anticipation of where his fingers were headed. As he slipped inside, he moaned, and I writhed helplessly against him.

I felt him watch my reaction, savoring the moment, and my head rocked into the pillow. Back arching, a moan escaped my lips as so many sensations flooded my body.

I gasped, pulling myself from the memory of our first time together and how it had been as if we were made for one another. Making love with Jaxon had been even more than I'd dreamed.

The memory of him, of us, couldn't be denied any longer. I was ready to grow, to move past the mistakes we'd made. It was time.

12

JAXON

In the distance, air pushed through a conch shell as someone's lips vibrated against the natural instrument. The loud, rich cry trumpeted and rose above the wind rustling through palm trees. The beat of a distant drum followed as the sun kissed the ocean in a blaze of red and orange. I leaned against my balcony railing far from but still a part of the sunset ceremony held on the beach until the last rays disappeared.

I was on a conference call with Xander, Jack, and Chris Shaw, another of the Gray Ghost team. There wasn't a lot I could do on my end, but if an opportunity arose to put an end to the militia group and keep the former and current SEALs safe, I would.

"Your parents got here a few hours ago," Chris confirmed. "They're using our phones, so they can't be tracked with theirs."

"Thank you," Xander and I said at the same time. Our parents would be safer in Maine with the Gray Ghost team. I cleared my throat. "Do you have any news on the rest of the former members of Dad's team?"

"We've managed to locate several, and they're in safe houses,"

Jack answered. "The rest are being tracked down, but the simple fact that we don't have a bead on them is good news."

Because if they didn't, then the enemy didn't either. The four of us talked for another ten or fifteen minutes before hanging up. An enormous weight lifted from my shoulders. The thought of harm coming to my parents was horrible. With their safety established, my hope was that Ty would come through on his end. Xander and I didn't talk about it much, but we both had assumed the militia group was also a part of the hostage abduction and why our brother was sent to South America on another mission.

Crossing my arms over the railing, I leaned over it to stare at the ocean. Kayla hadn't been surfing once since she'd been back here. That was something she'd loved to do when the three of us were close. She'd won several competitions. Kieran had been her biggest fan. I wondered if the lack of her brother's presence was why she wasn't actively pursuing Pipe.

I hung my head, appalled at the part I'd played in causing her pain. I vowed to do everything in my power to help her. When we were on the island, I would work on helping her rediscover why she loved to surf. Because when she was out there in the ocean, there were very few who could do it better.

The roar of the ocean matched the echo of her spirit as she rode the cresting waves. There was joy in watching her, an innate sense of freedom and synchronicity in the moments as she soared across a wave and it curved over her head.

———

Kayla

WITH JAXON BUSY talking with his brothers, I slipped into the bathroom. My phone had been vibrating on and off all morning. I knew who it was by the ringtone.

There were several texts in which Roy had threatened to find me and that it was only a matter of time. Of course, he'd worded them carefully, in a way that I couldn't use against him if I went to the police and filed a restraining order—no doubt he'd had practice at that. There was nothing that stated what he intended to do. It was the same with the voicemails.

My throat tightened as if his hand was around it, squeezing until it was nearly impossible to breathe. I could picture the crazed look in his eyes and conjure the same horror of realizing he would kill me as I had the last time we were together.

But he hadn't ended my life. Not that time. And given a reprieve, I would fight him with everything I had. When my phone vibrated with another one of his calls, I was ready.

"Hello, Roy." I kept my voice soft and even.

"I paid a visit to your parents' house, Kayla. You'll have to come home sooner or later. And when you do, I'll have you."

Bile climbed my throat, and my entire body shook with the horror of him around my parents. I'd left them vulnerable by not saying anything. But deep down, I didn't think he would harm them. It was me he was after. I forced myself to laugh mockingly. "You're not very smart. Don't you think I would have thought that's the first place you would go? You'll never find me."

Something crashed on his end, and I cringed, my fingers tingling from the death grip I had on my phone. I had to keep calm for just a few more seconds. Then I would hang up.

"I'm close, bitch, and when I find you, I'll drag you home by your hair."

"Yeah, that's not gonna happen." I crossed my fingers, hoping like hell I was right and that he'd never looked at Stephanie's flash drive. "I saw your handiwork on the news the other day, and the thing is, I have Stephanie's flash drive. If you come anywhere near my family or me, it goes straight to the cops, along with your career."

I gave him two seconds to respond then hung up and threw my phone into the bedroom, where it bounced on the mattress twice before settling.

It was as I'd hoped. He'd never bothered to look at the drive. I felt like the sands of time were slipping through my fingers. I had to see what she had stored there. *Please, Stephanie, have something I can use to put him away for life.*

13

KAYLA

The only other sound in the condo as I hunkered down in the guest room was Jaxon's muffled voice as he talked on the phone. With urgency, I dug through my bag until I found my laptop. The room, which was to be mine when my parents moved in, was done in relaxing gray tones with a hint of mauve tinting the white trim. A mix of pink and white shells lined the windowsill to bring more of the outside in. None of it worked to calm my frazzled nerves as I climbed onto the bed and pulled the computer in front of me, impatient for the screen to come to life.

Time was moving too quickly, and all the fine hairs on my body stood on end in anticipation that Roy would find me. I couldn't stay in the condo forever. I would have to go to my parents' to help them pack—*today*.

When it finally booted up, I plugged Stephanie's flash drive with the *Honolulu Star-Advisor* logo into the USB slot and opened the drive.

I scrolled through the files, which were organized by date, until I found the last month she'd saved anything. There were several assigned articles that she'd turned in for print... and one she hadn't. The only reason I knew that was because the title was "A Champion Inside the Ring, but What About Outside?"

With a click on the trackpad, the file opened. I scanned the long article, where she'd documented a brief background then Roy's rise to fame, his losses in the beginning, the consecutive wins, and finally the fight that had awarded him the championship belt.

Then the article took a dark turn about the champ's less than stellar behavior outside of the limelight. There had been rumors of abuse and rape, but the one or two who'd come forward had disappeared. The interview consisted of an anonymous source and Stephanie's testimony. *Holy shit.* It would go viral if published in the wake of her death, especially since it had been ruled a homicide because of the bruising found on her neck.

I should have taken pictures of my neck and cheek too. The humiliation had been so acute that I'd wanted to pretend it hadn't happened. The way he'd eroded my self-confidence had blindsided me. It was something I continued to struggle with, to rebuild, despite my bravado.

But no more. If I didn't do something to stop him, he would do it to another woman. I opened an email, addressed it to the head editor at the *Star-Advisor*, and gave a summary of what I'd found of Stephanie's, saying that I would turn over as evidence to the police but was giving the paper an exclusive too. I scheduled the email to send in two days. If something happened to me, it would still get into the right hands.

I set my computer aside. The condo was quiet. Jaxon must have been off the phone. Not wanting to deal with any more of Roy's calls or texts, I left my cell on my bed and went in search of Jaxon.

He was in the living room with a glass of amber liquid, probably whiskey. I sat next to him, hoping to ease into my difficult story. "How'd it go with your brothers?"

"As well as expected. With our parents safe, I was able to

convince Xander to stay on his honeymoon. They'll move to another location, making sure not to use social media or credit cards. At least not his."

"That's good." I took a deep breath and met his concerned gaze. "I'm ready to tell you everything."

He didn't say anything, just waited for me to continue.

With as much detail as I could manage, I recounted how Roy and I had dated, and told him the little things that had been easy to make excuses for because I hadn't wanted to admit it was happening. Violence wasn't something I'd experienced. It was as if it wasn't quite real. But he'd made it very much so.

"The day I left, we fought, and he struck me so hard that I went down to the floor. He followed." I waved to my neck. "I thought I was going to die, had even lost consciousness. When he went out, not long after, I packed everything I owned and took off."

Jaxon drew me to him. Barely leashed violence radiated from him in that quiet, controlled way he had. But with him, I would never be afraid—he'd only ever protected me.

"Has he been calling, texting?" He pressed a kiss to the top of my head.

"Yes. Tonight, I answered and returned his threat with one of my own."

His hand stilled, and it was as if the room paused with him. "Tell me."

I twisted so my side was against his and drew my knees up. His arms still encircled me, keeping the darkness at bay. "I found a company flash drive at Roy's and took it with me. Tonight, I finally looked at it. Stephanie was a reporter at the same paper as me and had written an article about Roy."

"Does the article point to him as a suspect?"

"It does."

"You know we need to take that into the station and put a warrant out for his arrest."

"I do. I should have opened it sooner. I wish I had. There's another thing. He said he's watching my parents' house."

Jax swore, and some of the weight I'd carried siphoned away. He would help. I didn't know why I'd been so ashamed, so stubborn, and not confided in him immediately.

"I'll call dispatch and see if I can get someone stationed in from of their home or increase the patrols, at the very least. And Kayla?" He waited, and I knew it was for me to take in his tone's seriousness before he continued. "Please don't leave the condo unless we're together. I can't risk anything happening to you."

I sunk my teeth into my bottom lip. I couldn't make that promise, but I was scared enough to take what he asked of me into consideration. He needed to know what else I'd planned. "I copied the article onto my computer and also scheduled an email to go to the paper for them to print it in two days."

"Let's go get it logged in as evidence, then."

His muscles tensed to stand, but I splayed my hand against his chest, freezing him in place. "Not tonight. Let's take care of it tomorrow."

Heat raced up my arm where my fingers lay over his heart then spread like wildfire. When I tilted my head so that our gazes met, I dropped the shields I'd been hiding behind and let him see the burning need I had for him, which I'd futilely tried to fight.

He reacted instantly, and his pupils expanded. When his arms loosened, I had a moment of insecurity.

"Come here." His voice was low and husky. Then his large hands grasped my hips, and when he lifted me, I straddled him. My hands rested against his broad shoulders, and I felt the power I had in that position.

I couldn't wait for him and pressed my lips to his, teasing. The connection between us sparked. Fiery need turned demanding. Our tongues tangled. His hands slipped from my hips to my back, and he drew me closer, so there was no space between us. Our kiss raged almost out of control until he slowed the pace then rested his forehead against mine.

"Kayla." My heart fluttered at how he said my name as if it was a prayer.

I could have lost myself in him with one touch of his hand.

"Sleep with me tonight. Let me hold you." I nodded, and he stood, lifting me with him in one powerful motion. Lying in his arms was where I wanted to be.

14

KAYLA

Morning came quickly, with bright rays shining through the windows Jaxon and I had left open. I moved through the kitchen in a cloud of happiness. The day promised clear skies. The waves called to me, but surfing would have to wait. That was something I wanted to do with Jaxon once I resolved the mess with Roy. Then there was my parents' move.

We had a lot going on.

The night before, I'd slept in Jaxon's bed, and I'd even woken in his arms. But that was as far as we'd taken things, and I was glad for it. I wanted to be with him, but I'd been vulnerable after sharing the details of my final minutes with Roy. Jaxon understood. Instead of using our intense connection to take things further, he'd comforted me, which I'd needed most. We were in the beginning stages of a relationship, something I'd always wanted with him but never allowed myself after Kieran.

After Jaxon had a cup of coffee with me, he went to work. It was his last week. We hadn't talked in depth about what would happen to us when he moved. I knew we would, though. Things were moving quickly, but we had so much history that it felt natural for us.

Jaxon and I had switched cars because Roy knew what I drove. I wasn't supposed to go to my parents' house alone. I spread strawberry jelly on a piece of toast and took a bite. I never promised to stay here. I planned to stop at the hardware store to get a smaller roller for the bathroom, which was close to the Coffee Hut, which was a bonus. I could get a mocha latte.

After a glance at the time to make sure the hardware store was open, I put my hair in a ponytail, grabbed my largest pair of sunglasses and my purse, and headed out. Once I was on the street in Jaxon's Escalade with the windows down, my outlook on the day rose considerably, and the worry over Roy retreated to the far recesses of my mind.

It didn't take terribly long to get to the street to buy the painting roller and pop into the Coffee Hut, my reward for shopping in a hardware store. I would have liked to have left that little chore to Jax, since I avoided those stores as much as I could. The smell was weird, some combination of pine sawdust, rubber, and cleaning products. No thanks.

By some miracle, I found a parking spot only two blocks away. Once out of the car, I merged with the morning sidewalk crowd making their way to work or the shops. I was in and out of the store in under fifteen minutes. With my purchase in hand, I walked the short distance to get my reward, practically salivating for the treat.

The bag crinkled against the door handle as I pushed it open and stepped inside. The scent of rich coffee beans infused the inviting space. It was a popular place that many of the people I'd grown up with frequented. I loved everything about the atmosphere, from the dark-wood ceiling and brick feature walls to the soft lighting and relaxed vibe.

Most of the tables were taken, which was fine. I planned to get my heaven-in-a-cup to go. I placed my order then went to wait by the live-wood counter off to the side.

"Kayla?"

I turned toward the vaguely familiar voice and froze for a brief moment at the sight of a beautiful pregnant woman. "Leslie? Oh, wow, you look great! And"—I motioned with my hand toward her basketball of a stomach—"When did this happen?" *Does my brother somehow know? Is that why he keeps appearing?*

She grinned. She'd always had the best smile—she glowed—and I couldn't help but feel happy along with her. But inside, I was shaken. I hadn't seen her since the accident.

"This happened seven months ago. My husband and I live an hour away but are here to spend some time with my parents before the baby's born."

"Well, congratulations. I'm so happy for you." And I meant it.

"Thanks." They called her order, and she left my side for a second to get her tea then returned. "Did you go to Kieran's bonfire?" Her eyes misted, and there was a slight tremble to her bottom lip, but she hid it by taking a sip of her drink.

So many emotions washed over me in a tidal wave. "I did. It had been a while. I was surprised by how many people there were."

She shrugged. "I'm not. Kieran was… everything. If you didn't know him, you wanted to. If you did, he was someone you looked up to, loyal, an inspiration. There isn't a day that goes by that I don't miss him. He was my best friend and the love of my life." Her gaze darted to the side then back. "I don't mean that I don't love my husband. I do. He's incredible, and I'm very happy. I just wanted you to know—"

"It's okay." I put my hand on her arm to stop her. "I understand. I was there, remember?"

"Yeah." She inhaled a long breath, and pain flashed across her features before she smoothed her hand over her stomach. "This would have been Kieran and me. That night…" She took a moment to gain control of her shaky voice while I waited patiently. "The night of the accident, I lost my entire world. I was pregnant, and we were going..." She choked on a sob, and I wrapped my arms around her while her confession screamed inside my head.

"Leslie, I had no idea. I'm so sorry." The loss of Kieran, the sister I would have had, and the niece or nephew shredded me.

She pulled back first. "With this pregnancy, I'm overly emotional." She wiped the tears away with trembling fingers. "I'll always love Kieran. This baby is a second chance for me, and I'm lucky to have it. And Matt. Speaking of Matt, I've got to meet him, or he'll worry and come looking for me." Her hand tightened around my arm in a brief squeeze. "It was so good to see you again, Kayla."

"It was so good to see you, too, Leslie. I've thought of you over the years."

The bell over the door jingled, and Leslie glanced over her shoulder. A large man walked in, scanning the room until he found Leslie, and he visibly relaxed. That inner glow she always had brightened, and she waved him over. He looked like a linebacker. But when he got to her side, there was such love and tenderness in the way he drew her to his side and brushed a kiss across her forehead. Longing for a love like that made me ache for Jaxon. There were so many wasted years. We could have had that if things hadn't gone so terribly wrong.

When he extended his hand to me, I shook it. As Leslie made introductions, recognition widened his easygoing smile.

"You resemble him." His deep voice rumbled. "Leslie's told me about you and Kieran and shared pictures. I'm glad for the chance to meet you."

I swallowed past the tightness in my throat. "It's wonderful to meet you as well, Matt."

We chatted for a few minutes, and my heart swelled with the knowledge that Kieran lived on with Leslie, since she'd shared him with her husband. Given the way they interacted and his acceptance of what she'd had and lost with my brother, I was truly happy for her. It seemed she'd healed in ways I never had.

After they left for her parents' house, I took my to-go cup of coffee and climbed into Jaxon's SUV. *Had Kieran told Jaxon about the baby?* Conflicting emotions warred in me about him knowing something about my brother that I hadn't known.

15

KAYLA

I drove to his place, rode the elevator, and let myself in on autopilot. The bag from the hardware store sat unopened on the island, and I wandered out onto the lanai to drink my coffee and wait for Jaxon to return for lunch.

As the minutes passed, I curled onto the patio chair, taking small sips of my coffee while confused emotions formed into anger. Neither my brother nor Jaxon had told me anything—and he had to have known. It was another layer of secrets and lies. And that night... there shouldn't have been anything between us after that. He should have told me. The hurt and annoyance with my brother was one thing, but Jaxon had become my lover that night.

By the time the door opened, and he appeared beside me, my emotions were turning into a raging fire.

I think my head swiveled like the girl's did in *The Exorcist* when I turned to look at him. I caught a flash of panic beneath the worry flashing through his usually hypnotizing brown eyes.

"Do you ever think of that night we'd spent together?" I didn't let him answer. "I do. More often than I should. You were my first. It meant something. I thought things had changed between us in those moments. You told me that I was your world, that we'd find a way to make my brother understand. But it wasn't true, was it? I mean, how could we make it work, build something epic together, when you were keeping so many secrets from me about my brother and Leslie?" I was shaking by the time I finished.

He didn't even try to come near me, and that sliced through the anger like a shard of glass. Instead, he sat on the chair next to me, running the palms of his hands over his face. When he lifted his gaze to mine, pain and resignation halted anything else I was going to say.

"I wanted to tell you. I'd argued with Kieran earlier that night about what he was doing. I didn't fully agree with their decision. There was no need to elope. Both their families loved them and would have supported them. But they'd made up their minds."

What the... "Elope?"

Wariness overshadowed the resignation he wore. "What were you referring to?"

My spine straightened, and my shoulders went back. "Uh-uh, no. You and my brother owe me. He's always so cryptic when he talks to me, and you have no excuse. You're here."

With his elbows on his thighs, he dropped his arms so his hands dangled over his knees and leaned forward. "What are you talking about?"

"Oh, no." I shook my head. "We are talking about all the secrets *you've* kept from me."

His gaze bounced between my eyes before he sighed, running his fingers through his hair, mussing it into that sexy just-woke-up look that I refused to let distract me.

"All right. Let's do this, then." He dropped his hands and leaned forward once more. "When Leslie found out she was pregnant, they were a mess. Kieran had that full-ride football scholarship, and Leslie had her own for academics. They were excited about college."

"I remember." They would have made it, eventually marrying as soon as they graduated. They had that once-in-a-lifetime kind of love that was equally enviable and inspiring.

"Kieran wouldn't listen. He and Leslie had made up their minds to get married. I was supposed to meet them the next morning to be a witness. They were driving to a bed and breakfast along the coast. No one else knew. I'd planned to tell you that morning, to bring you with."

"Then they crashed." Leslie had been thrown from the car, which, oddly enough, saved her life but not the baby's. My brother had gone over the cliff with the car and died on impact.

"Yeah." He stood then started pacing. "They had everything planned out. How she'd take that first year off, deferring her scholarships so she could spend the time with their baby. He wasn't going to live in the football house but instead get one of the apartments on campus for married couples. He was good enough to get drafted into the NFL. They hadn't figured everything out, but they thought they could get a nanny to help the second year. That way, Leslie could start college, and he'd hoped you would be there too. They both knew you would lend a hand any way you could."

Tears streamed down my cheeks. I would have done anything for my brother. My heart shattered all over again. "Why did he keep this from me?"

"It was all a shock." Jaxon sat next to me.

All the anger and jealousy I'd felt dissolved. I imagined how huge it all must have had been and how they must've been doing what they thought was best. They were focused only on each other.

My body jerked before I swallowed down the tears. I could hold onto hurt outrage over their secret pact from so long ago, or I could try to move past it. If I held on, I would lose Jaxon all over again because I'd be forced to walk away. In my heart, I know that wasn't what I wanted. We were young, and while he should have confessed as soon as I walked back into his life, I sort of understood why he hadn't. So I let him hold me.

"Then we happened. I'd wanted you for so long, but you were two years younger. It wasn't until you were a freshman that I would even let myself entertain the possibility of anything other than friendship."

I slumped against him, letting his confession sink in. So many years. We'd wasted so much time. "Why didn't you tell me after?"

He rubbed my arm in soothing circles. "You were wrecked when he died. And you attributed some of the blame from not knowing what had happened to me."

"Because of the overnight bags found at the crash site. You knew things I didn't. It didn't sit well then and still doesn't."

"I know, and I'm sorry." He pressed a kiss to the top of my head, and I shut my eyes. "I'd planned to tell him about us. But the next day never came like it was supposed to."

There was too much to process. Instead, I allowed myself to feel his strength, his warmth. He lifted me so that I was cradled in his arms and sitting on his lap.

"What did you mean about Kieran talking to you?"

Emotionally exhausted, I answered his next question without thought. "He visits me." With that, we had no more secrets between us, and I wondered if it would finally be our time for an epic relationship.

16

JAXON

Kayla's words ran through my head on my lunch break as I ate a BLT in front of the TV. She was next to me on the couch, her legs curled under her, but she was quiet, letting me digest that she saw Kieran and they had actual conversations—even though he was dead. It was a lot to take in but not completely unbelievable. I'd seen too much in the Navy and on overseas missions to discount what she'd told me.

A red banner flashed across the TV: Breaking News. I watched as men and women poured off a plane. Tired and unkempt, their looks of relief tinged with worry and grief were unmistakable. I grabbed the remote and turned up the volume. The reporter explained that the deplaning people were US Embassy staff forced to leave the country by the Venezuelan president's order.

They hadn't all returned. Five members were reported missing with no word on their safety.

"That's what Tyler is doing." The Navy must have learned of the hostages and sent a team in to locate them.

"Oh, no." Kayla lay a hand on my arm as my cell rang.

Xander's name came up on the screen. "Hey."

"Are you watching the news?"

I grunted. "Yeah."

"We know where Ty is." Xander's voice cut through my thoughts.

I huffed out a sigh. "It's better than not knowing. And at least this time, we don't have to worry about faulty intel." I hoped. So many things could go wrong.

"I'd like to convince myself of that too. Any word from Mark? Or from the police or higher up?"

"Nothing that we haven't already discussed." We talked for another couple of minutes about the militia group, both of us worried about our brother.

Kayla squeezed my arm as she got up, taking the dishes with her. The water turned on in the kitchen, the sounds of her rinsing then putting the plates in the dishwasher in the background. Then she grabbed her laptop, went out onto the lanai, and closed the sliding door with a click behind her. She had some work to do for the paper, a book review to write. And she'd given me some privacy to talk to my brother.

I rubbed my hand over my forehead. I had a bad feeling about Ty. I couldn't shake it. Xander had the same instinct that something was wrong or about to implode.

There wasn't much more we could say or do, so I switched the topic. "How's Riley doing?"

"She loves it here. We've made plans to come back next year. What's going on with you and Kayla? Is she still at your place?"

"She is." I didn't want to get into everything. There was enough worry between the two of us over Ty and our parents. "I'm moving in a couple of weeks, close to when you and Riles are back. I'm planning on bringing Kayla with me."

"It's like that, huh?" I could hear the smile in Xander's voice.

"It's been like that since we were in high school. All that's left is convincing her. She's the one. She always has been."

"It's about damn time, Jax. And Riles will love her."

That was what I was counting on. "There will be times we won't be around if we have work to do for the Gray Ghost team. It'll be nice that they aren't alone on the island."

"I agree. Ty's keeping the condo for all of us, though. If they wanted, they could stay there when we're away, so they're not so vulnerable."

"They could. I'm counting on Jack not needing both of us at the same time. And Ty will probably re-up when his term is done. I haven't heard otherwise. I think he has a year or two before that happens."

"A lot can happen in a year. You never know what he'll do." Xander echoed the thoughts that were swirling in my head.

I hoped the reason Xander hadn't re-upped again wasn't because all hell broke loose after an information leak. I worried about our brother making it out of Venezuela in one piece.

After tossing the phone back onto the coffee table, I opened the sliding glass doors. Kayla was typing on her laptop, so I waited until she looked up.

Her bright-green eyes met mine, and I felt as if she could see into my soul. *We'll be okay. She just needs time.*

"Want to watch a movie? Have a low-key night?"

A slight smile curved her lips. "Only if I get to pick it."

"I know I'm going to regret this, but sure."

A wicked laugh burst from her as she closed the laptop. "You make the popcorn, and I'll cue up a romantic comedy." She rubbed her hands together as she brushed past me and grabbed the remote. "Get ready for a night of them."

I went into the kitchen to get the snacks ready, happy that even though she hadn't voiced it, she was on her way to forgiving me.

17

KAYLA

The sun that morning had been a giant orange beacon as it rose from the arms of the ocean. I marveled at its power. I'd lain in bed in Jaxon's equally powerful embrace. It was getting harder to resist the palpable desire between us, but I wasn't emotionally ready after learning the secrets he'd kept all those years. I did, however, understand, and time and his continued patience would heal the hurt that lingered.

After Jaxon had left, I'd showered, had breakfast, then painted the master bathroom, determined to get at least one thing checked off the list. While I ran the roller up and down the walls, my mind wandered, something still nagging me after my conversation with Leslie.

We'd buried Kieran wearing the beaded necklace that Leslie had given him. But at the scene of the accident, not far from where Leslie lay, there had been a shark's-tooth necklace, the same one that the cheerleaders had presented to the football team.

Leslie didn't have one, and Kieran's was with the pictures in the small wooden box that I'd taken from his room.

Kieran's words of warning about Roy filtered back to me:

"He's coming for you, Little K, and you've got to be ready. Don't have your head in the sand like I did." *What had he meant with that last part? Had he known the person who'd forced them off the road?*

The police had never found the driver, and it had been ruled a hit-and-run. The only clue I had was the duplicate necklace—we'd all assumed it was Kieran's. I wished the cheerleaders had put the guys' names or charms with their uniform numbers on them.

In the kitchen, I cleaned the roller then wiped down the sink, so there weren't any traces of splattered paint. Setting the tools aside to dry, I grabbed my purse and slipped my feet into sandals. I had a little time before Jaxon would be home. I sent him a quick text, letting him know that I was going to see Mateo at the auto shop where he worked.

Be careful, he replied.

We were going to my parents' that afternoon to help them pack up the house. The only concession I'd made to them was that I wouldn't go there alone, since Roy was probably staked out somewhere waiting for me. A shiver coursed through my body at the thought of my ex and how in a physical confrontation, I was powerless against him. I didn't carry a gun. Jaxon did. And even though Roy was all swollen muscle and nasty attitude, I'd put my money on Jaxon's skills any day. His SEAL training had prepared him for virtually any situation.

He'd left me his SUV again—*thank you*—and I got behind the wheel of the fully loaded vehicle. It sucked for him to be driving my bare-bones Honda Civic. Once on the street and stopped at a light, I slipped my oversized sunglasses on and a baseball hat, pulling my hair through the small opening in the back. Roy wouldn't think to look at other cars, at least not unless he spotted me, and I wasn't going to make it easy for him with my appearance. Besides, the auto shop wasn't anywhere near my parents' house.

I pulled into the crowded parking lot for the auto shop about half an hour later. The garage doors were up, and I could see a couple of guys working on cars. Two were up on the lifts, and one wasn't. I got out and crossed over to the open bays. Mateo was bent over the engine of an older model black Mustang.

The smell of oil, dust, and tires saturated the space, and I stepped inside with care.

Mateo turned and smiled. "Hey, Kayla." He wiped some of the grease from his hands onto a rag near his hip.

"Hi, Mateo." One of the other mechanics stopped what he was doing, and I felt his eyes on me. "Do you have a minute?"

"Sure. Is there a problem with your car?"

"No. Um, I wanted to talk to you about something."

"Sure." He waved over to a picnic table set off to the side of the lot. "We can go there."

We walked in silence. I perched on the bench after he straddled it. *How to ask him this...* I nibbled on my lip, contemplating the best approach.

"Is everything okay?" His brows furrowed.

"Sort of." I was going for it. "Not really. I keep thinking about how Kieran died and how the other driver was never found."

"Yeah, that sucks. I'm sure it's hard for your family." Gone was his customary laid-back-surfer aura. Concern tugged his lips down, and a seriousness I'd rarely seen etched itself into his eyes.

"You and Kieran were close." I blew out a breath, forcing the tension in my shoulders to ease. "Do you remember anyone on the team not liking him?"

"Kieran?" His brows raised. "No way. He was the team captain. Everyone looked up to him. And he was a great friend."

I lay my hand on his arm. "I'm not questioning you. I remember you and a couple of others were in his inner circle.

The thing I'm unsure of is whether there was anyone who resented him or acted differently after he died."

Mateo shook his head, and a thick black tuft of hair fell across his forehead and partially obscured one of his eyes until he swiped it back, smearing a streak of grease in its wake. "Yeah, no. I don't remember anyone acting oddly. His death was a devastating loss to all of us."

"It was." I fought the emotion and offered a small smile. "That's all I wanted to know. I've got to get to my parents' in an hour."

He stood when I did, and we walked to the middle of the lot, pausing when by Jaxon's SUV. He took a step toward the car he'd been working on, and I grinned. "Is that your old car?" I seemed to remember that it was dark gray, not black.

"Nah, but she's a beaut. I got rid of mine shortly after high school."

I let my gaze wander over the classic lines of the older Mustang. "Such a great car."

"It is. I have a stripped-down version I'm rebuilding at home when I have spare time."

"It fits you." My phone beeped with a text, and I gave him a small wave. "Thanks again, Mateo." I used the key fob to unlock the car as someone pulled into the lot. I slid behind the wheel just as Vivi pulled into the spot next to mine. She got out of her car, all smiles. I gave her a little wave as Mateo's parting words reached me.

"Always good to see you, Little K."

Once I buckled in, I dug in my purse for my phone, my fingers closing around it just as it rang, glad my windows were up so I wouldn't have to chat with Vivi.

"Hi." It was my mom.

"Aloha, Kayla." Her warm voice came through the connection like a hug, and I grinned, relaxing against the car's leather seat. "I wanted to let you know there was a man here, looking for you."

Oh shit. White-hot panic shot through me like lightning. "Who was it?"

"He said his name was Roy. He didn't leave a way to get ahold of him, but he said he'd be back. I let him know you'd be over later today."

"Okay. Thanks, Mom. I'll see you soon."

"Bye, sweetheart."

My hands shook as I swiped the screen to check my texts. Roy didn't disappoint, and I stared at his text in horror: *Until this afternoon.*

Holy hell.

I needed Jaxon's help.

18

JAXON

y entire body was strung tight with worry over the possible terrorist strike and the ex-boyfriend stalking Kayla, but at least telling her the secret I'd held for so many years had gone better than I'd hoped. She was still here and willing to give us a try. It was more than I thought I would ever have with her.

When I unlocked the door to my condo and stepped inside, it was to Kayla pacing the length of the living room. Something was very wrong. "Kayla?"

"Oh, God." She whirled around, and the naked fear in her eyes almost brought me to my knees.

"What's happened?" I closed the distance between us. My fingers curled around her shoulders, and I held her at arm's length.

"Roy was at my parents' door! He spoke to them." She shook beneath my touch as she told me her mom called about Roy stopping by and that he would be back this afternoon when she was coming over. He'd followed with a text saying he would see her soon. "What am I going to do?"

"We're going to the station and turning over the evidence,

and you'll make a statement about Roy. While you're doing that, I'm going to comb the area with several cops and look for him. You'll be safe there until I come back for you."

"No." She jerked back, putting some distance between us. "I can't. My parents, Jax. What if he hurts them?"

I ran my hands through my hair. *Shit.* I understood where she was coming from, and it would have been my first reaction, too, to get them to safety. "I'll talk to your dad. Get him to take your mom away for a few days before he goes back to work."

She wrung her hands, nodding as she processed. "Okay. Yeah, that would work." Shame pulled her features tight as she turned to me. "Are you going to tell him about Roy, about what he's capable of?"

"I am." That was non-negotiable. "He'll know something is wrong. The best way to get them out of the house is to tell him the truth. Once he's assured that I'll protect you, he'll want your mom far away and safe." I grasped her arm in a light hold and pulled her to me. "It's going to be okay."

A tremor ran through her before she did what I knew she would—she dug deep and put her game face on. Kayla was nothing if not strong and resilient.

"After they leave, I want to go there with you. So long as there isn't a Roy sighting, we'll get the packing done as promised. It's important, and the sooner they're out of there, they're a little closer to their retirement years." She drew a deep breath. "And the memories. They're good ones, but it's hard to walk by Kieran's room, to feel him in every inch of that house, and they're living it. They need this fresh start."

"Go sit on the balcony, and I'll get things taken care of in here."

Rising onto her toes, she pressed a kiss on my lips that I very much wanted to deepen. But first things first—I needed to call her dad. He was going back on Monday, which would be my last day. Kayla and I had to talk about what came next. I knew what

I wanted, but I worried that she might not want the same. Aside from the ex-boyfriend issues, she had another life miles from me, and I wasn't sure she was willing to move.

Her dad was worried about Kayla but agreed to get his wife to safety so long as I remained glued to Kayla's side if she left my condo. He made that my official duty, as opposed to the usual beat cop tasks I had. And while Kayla was relatively protected in my condo, she was like a caged bird. I didn't know if she would do as I asked, so what her dad ordered was fine by me. I wouldn't be able to concentrate away from her, anyway. To be extra safe, I asked to install a tracking app on her phone. I was thankful that she let me.

She wanted to wait to turn the flash drive over as evidence. We got lunch together, and I joined her outside, where we would talk about the next steps.

There wasn't a cloud in the sky, and the sun sparkled off the water like diamonds. When all this was behind us, I wanted to spend hours with Kayla at the shore, chasing the best waves, and later, holding her in my arms throughout the night. I wanted to go to sleep with her and have her be the first thing I saw every morning. We had a lot of lost time to make up for.

"Thanks." With her legs tucked under her, a tentative smile curved her lips as she took the proffered sandwich. "Before you say anything, I know I need to take the flash drive to the station. But I'm terrified for my parents and would rather do it tomorrow. Roy says he's watching my house, but he knows what I have, and I would think he would alternate from staking out the house to the police station, making sure I don't deliver any incriminating evidence. It's one day, and I will feel immensely better once my parents are away and safe."

"Do you have the flash drive on you or in your purse?"

"No. I don't want to risk him taking it from me. It's in the small wooden box of Kieran's in my room here."

I nodded in agreement. "Your parents will be gone in about

an hour and a half. They're going up the coast to a bed and breakfast that your mom loves."

"Thank you." She visibly relaxed. "I hope this is over soon."

That was my cue. "I'll agree to making a statement and turning the evidence over tomorrow so long as we don't go to your parents' to pack until after that. You're safer here, and there are things we need to discuss."

"Oh. That's never good. Should I be worried?"

I set my plate down next to hers on the small table and rested my forearms on my legs, leaning forward. "No, of course not. I'm the one who's worried."

"Why?"

I grinned at her. She always had been impatient. "I know what we have between us is fairly new, but our history isn't." I clasped our hands together. "We've known each other all our lives, and for more than half of the time, I thought of you as mine. I love you, Kayla, and I want to take things further."

A blinding smile altered her face from beautiful to stunning. "I love you, too, Jaxon. I never stopped."

The tension between my shoulders eased, and I dove into what I feared she wouldn't agree to next. "You already know I sold this place and will be moving. When your dad convinced me to try out being a beat cop to see if that's the next step for me, I thought it might be. But it's not what I want to do. I want you to know everything you'd be getting into if you make a commitment to me."

"I do know you." Her brows furrowed. "What does it matter if you're a cop or not?"

"Because there will be times I'm not home, when I'm back on missions. Dangerous ones. I've been in contact with a buddy of mine, a former Navy SEAL who owns Gray Ghost Security. They do rescue and recovery, among other jobs. I wouldn't work for them full time but mission specific and when they need more men."

"Okay. That's not too different from what you were doing as a SEAL. What you're telling me is that I'd be alone sometimes. I've known you forever, Jax, and going on missions, being a hero, is part of who you are. There aren't limits to what I'll accept about you. I love everything about you. I'm willing to adapt and to do what it takes to make a life with you work."

Goddamn. This woman. She was everything to me. I stood and pulled her into my arms, needing to feel more of her. After a few seconds, I told her everything. "There's more. I'm moving into one of the houses on the island that my mom's family's owned for generations. You remember it, right? You were there once or twice."

"Sure. It's beautiful."

"Xander and his new wife will be living there when they're back from their honeymoon. Riley's great. I know you'll like her." I loosened my arms so I could gauge her reaction. "Xander signed on with the Gray Ghosts too. But we're going to start a custom-surfboard business."

"On the island?" She tilted her head to the side, weighing what I'd dumped on her.

"Yes. There would be a place for you in the business if you wanted it, but there's no pressure. You've always loved to read, and I get that your job is perfect for you. Are you able to work remotely?"

"Yes."

Her carefree laugh filled the balcony, urging me to ask my next question. "The point to all of this is that I was hoping you'd move in with me on that island."

"I would love to live with you." When her arms wound around my neck, I lifted her. She wrapped her legs around my waist, and I held her tightly. For the first time in years, I was where I should have been.

19

KAYLA

Jaxon's arms banded around me, and I swore my soul sighed. He had been my childhood crush and my teen obsession, and over the years, I'd thought of him as an unattainable dream. In his embrace, all my feelings for him melded into an unbreakable bond, one I wouldn't let petty differences destroy.

With him, I was home. Safe. Loved and cherished. I wanted it more than I could ever have expressed.

One of Jaxon's hands moved to cradle my head as he deepened the hungry kiss, our tongues tangling together. I couldn't get close enough. The clothes between us were a barrier I wanted gone.

When he broke the kiss, I swayed in his arms. In slow motion, he peeled off my T-shirt. My bra followed. I tugged at his shirt, and he took a step back, pulling it over his head by the back—so sexy. My fingers traced the swell and dip of his defined chest. I was barely aware of him divesting us of the rest of our clothes until he pulled me close, skin on skin.

When his hand cupped the back of my neck, tilting my head once again for his kiss, I followed his lead willingly. He backed us against a wall then, with a hand beneath me, lifted me. I wrapped my legs around his waist while he continued to support me. Our kiss heated, turning frantic—even more so than when we were young.

When we broke apart, he nibbled on my lower lip as I sucked in air I hadn't realized I needed. He trailed kisses down my neck, biting at the apex of my shoulder and sending jolts of desire to my already aching core.

I kneaded his shoulders, whimpering. It wasn't enough. He had me trapped in that position, and I couldn't do all I wanted to. On a growl, he pulled me against him, and in the next second, we were striding into the bedroom. With infinite care, he lowered me to his mattress, following me down. I welcomed his weight.

We played a silent game of tug of war while I attempted to gain the position to sit astride him. He grinned. "Next round."

I couldn't help the laugh that escaped because there would be a next time and so many more after that. Jaxon was attentive and wild. I was more than fine with his weight over me, making me feel more than I'd ever experienced. Even more than our only night together—we were kids then. Now, I had the man, and I wasn't letting him go.

His hand cupped my breast, and I arched as his tongue swirled around the stiff peak of my nipple. My skin heated as my breath sawed in and out. I needed him to fill me. My fingers curled around his thickness, relishing his answering moan.

"Not yet." He gently removed my hand.

Frustration itched along my body. He shifted, moving lower. Goosebumps erupted where he no longer covered me. Then he spread my legs and settled between them. I gasped at the first brush of his tongue. His teeth nipped gently at my nub, the pads of his fingers following, caressing and rubbing in conjunction with the overwhelming explosion of his fingers filling me. My back arched in response. Everything faded except for his touch.

He made me crazy. Sensation after sensation shot from his mouth to my core, heating every inch of me. A fine sheen of perspiration coated my skin with each rolling wave of desire crashing over me. Deep inside, he hooked his finger while his mouth stimulated that bundle of nerves, and my body exploded. He groaned, covering me fully with his mouth.

When the light show eased behind my eyelids, the pulsing of my core rippled. I needed him like my next breath. "Please." I couldn't form any other words but tugged on his large shoulders. "I need you."

He shifted, and I whimpered from the loss, my body loose, relaxed, but also desperate for more of him. We weren't finished. Not by a long shot. There was the crinkle of a condom wrapper, and then he was over me, his lips full and slick from tasting me. Another jolt of need hit me hard at the sight of this incredibly handsome man. Our eyes met, and I gasped at the hunger reflected in his gaze, the fierce desire.

"Are you sure, Kayla?" His voice was rough with want, his body tense with barely restrained need.

I moaned when he pressed at my entrance. He held still, waiting for my response. "Yes," I whimpered again. When he didn't move, frustration had me digging my nails into his hips, pulling him closer and growling. "Jax!"

He chuckled, dipped his head, and nipped at the edge of my jaw. "I'll never get enough of you."

Then he was inside me, thrusting deep, and I wasn't capable of thought, only feeling. He loomed over me, and I matched the movement of hips with my own. His broad shoulders flexed above me, sexy as hell. Explosions rocked my body, and I screamed his name. When the last tremor quieted, my body went limp, sated. We lay together for several minutes, catching our breath, coming down from the mind-numbing sensations. Then his grip shifted and wrapped around my waist, and he rolled, taking me with him.

Sprawled over him, our legs tangled, my fingers tracing lazy circles over his washboard stomach, I was content.

"There have been so many nights I've dreamed of holding you in my arms again."

I wanted to nod because I felt the same. But the movement was more than my exhausted body could handle. "I never found anyone to love like what I have for you. No one could even come close." And they hadn't. I'd given my heart to him years before.

"I love you, Kayla."

My eyelids fluttered until I couldn't hold them open any longer, and I whispered that I loved him too. In his arms, I drifted to sleep, finally home.

20

KAYLA

With my hands wrapped around a steaming cup of coffee, I sat on the cushioned chaise lounge on the lanai, watching the sun rise in a fiery burst of orange and pink as it separated from the arms of the ocean to climb the sky.

We'd woken slowly and made love a second time. As a result, my languid body was one with the lounger I reclined on. He was everything I'd remembered and so much more. Mature Jaxon was worth waiting for.

There was a lot left for us to discuss, especially the blame I'd placed on him and the hurt from the distance we'd both retreated into. But I knew we would heal all our old wounds and be stronger from them, as we'd come so far already.

The chair next to me groaned as Jaxon lowered himself into it, a twin cup of coffee in his hand. "You ready for today?"

"As ready as I'll ever be." He was talking about going to the station with him. I would have rather had the topic of moving to the island, especially because it would have been a better place to hide from Roy, but that was a week or two in the future. Our hope was that the article Stephanie had written and my statement would be enough evidence for an arrest warrant and that Roy would be picked up sooner rather than later.

"It'll be fine. I'll be right there with you, and after your statement is taken and the evidence logged, we'll come back here."

"Yeah, let's get this over with, then." I gulped my last sip then stood. "I've been slacking on the painting." He grinned, and my knees went weak. I suspected it would always be like that, since I had that reaction to him even when we were kids.

"I'll be off this afternoon, and I'll help. There isn't much to do, just the living room and kitchen. We can knock out the rest of it today." His grin turned wolfish, and butterflies took flight in my stomach. "Come here."

In two steps, I was beside him. He took the empty mug from my hand, depositing it on the small table. Our clothes were next, falling around our feet. The hungry look in his eyes made my heart flutter. He leaned forward, brushing his fingers along the outside of my thigh. Trails of goosebumps followed in their wake.

When his hands settled on my hips, he guided me to straddle him, and I looped my arms around his neck. A nudge to the small of my back and I pressed fully to his solid chest, brushing my lips over his. For the time being, I controlled the pace. Tasting, teasing, until he took control, tangling our tongues together on a moan.

In a slow caress, his hand moved from the small of my back to cup the back of my head. He tilted my head for a better angle and deepened the kiss. I couldn't get close enough. Every inch of my body against his burned for more, for skin-on-skin contact.

I ground down on his hard length that pressed against the apex of my thighs, begging entrance. With a growl, he responded by flexing his hips and pushing up, hitting the exact spot I needed him to.

When he broke our kiss, I arched into him, my head falling

back as he rained kisses down the side of my neck. His teeth sunk into the curve where my neck and shoulder met at the same time as he pushed against me, sending a burst of sensations through my body. I cried out, light exploding behind my eyelids.

I floated in a cloud, tethered by his embrace.

My head was cradled against his chest as both of us regulated our breathing. The morning filtered back in slow increments, and I wanted to return to bed and spend the day with him there. But we had an unpleasant task to do.

When he stood, holding me to him, I let my legs slide down his body until my feet touched the floor. It was a dose of reality I wanted to fight against, especially when I stepped back, creating space between us. I felt the loss of him instantly, and I didn't like it.

"I'll grab a shower and my purse, and we can go." After a fast stop to the bathroom and a shower in record time, despite his joining me there, I slipped my feet into a pair of sandals and met him by the front door. Hand in hand, we rode the elevator then got into my car, since he'd driven it for a few days.

Traffic was thick on the way to the station, and we were quiet, each of us lost in our thoughts. Beside him, I felt safe. The usual worry I felt when I left his condo didn't exist, and soon, Roy would be behind bars.

The flash drive was in Jaxon's pocket, and I preferred it that way. Tomorrow, the newspaper would get the scheduled email and have the scoop on the story. I would let the officer who took my statement know that, too, so they could act immediately. If I didn't do this, not only would my life continue to be in danger, but some other unsuspecting woman would be hurt in the wake of falling for his charming side—the one that hid the monster.

As we pulled into the parking lot, a cacophony of nerves slammed into me. Not for who I would face inside, since I knew a lot of them because they worked with my dad, but because of what I would tell them. Dad was away at a bed and breakfast on our suggestion, but I had to make it right and give him and Mom the same story before one of his buddies told him.

After pulling into a spot and turning the engine off, Jax opened his door. I met him around the front of the car, and we trudged up the steps. But at the top, I tugged on his hand in a silent bid to wait.

"What is it?" He tucked a strand of my hair behind my ear, and I fought the urge to burrow into his arms.

I shook inside. It was a hard step.

Jax didn't push me but waited until I was ready to talk, a trait of his that I cherished. He had a wealth of patience and an innate understanding of my mercurial moods.

"I'm embarrassed. He hurt me. It makes me feel weak and stupid, even though I know I'm not. But I put myself in that situation. I stayed after he did it the first time." I'd never told him that Roy had slapped me before. I had been so shocked that I couldn't believe it had happened. I had been so emotionally distraught and mortified that when he apologized and promised he would never do it again, I grasped the lie like a lifeline.

But my confidence took a major hit that day. I hadn't known it, but he had been steadily chipping away at it until that last time. If I hadn't left, my future would have been bleak.

Jax pulled me into the warmth of his body, and I absorbed the comfort he offered. For several seconds, we stood that way, his hand smoothing the back of my hair in a soothing caress. "You have nothing to be ashamed of. Most of the guys in there will want his head for laying even a finger on you. We all understand the psychology behind the abuse. Coming here and sharing your story shows how strong you are."

I leaned back, and he brushed his lips across my forehead, taking a moment to breathe me in before we separated.

"Are you ready?" There was no pressure in his voice or body

language, and I knew he would give me all the time I needed to prepare. His patience and the love radiating from his touch did more for me than anything.

His hand firmly in mine, I nodded and stepped to his side. We walked into the station together, and I greeted those I knew. After a word to Charlie and concerned looks from those around us, I settled into the chair beside his desk. Jax pulled up a second and joined me. With him by my side and a deep, steadying breath, I unloaded my life with Roy.

Several officers surrounded us by the time we were done, anger swirling in their hard eyes and their jaws clenched. Stephanie's article was read and logged as evidence. An arrest warrant for attempted manslaughter was issued for Roy.

I was surprised by how cathartic it was to tell my story for the second time. Once Jax had slid the flash drive across the desk to Charlie, the burden I'd carried lessened substantially.

———

Jaxon

AFTER WE LEFT the police station, I drove Kayla back to the condo and walked her inside. Her steps had been lighter, her smile easier. It was the right thing to do, but I couldn't shake the unease that Roy was closing in. Leaving her side, even though she was behind the condo's locked and solid door, had been painful.

I didn't have a lot of time left at my job as a beat cop, and I was looking forward to when it would come to an end. Kayla and I would go to my family's island, where I could protect her better. Too bad Xander and Tyler weren't in residence. Sending her parents away had eased her worry, but I would have preferred that her father stayed. He was a formable adversary, should Roy try anything, heart surgery or not. But I understood her need to remove them from harm's way because of the tragedy they'd suffered when Kieran died.

I pulled into my parking space, and as soon as I got out of the car, Mrs. Malone, one of the other tenants in the building, walked by with her tiny chihuahua. I waved just as a beetle scuttled past us, sending the dog into a frenzy of yapping barks.

"Oh, I'm sorry, dear." She tugged her dog away from the bug and urged him toward the entrance to the street. "Milo hates bugs."

I smiled at the older woman and headed for the elevator as my phone rang. It was Mark, Ty's friend who worked as an analyst in support of the SEAL team. Alarm spiked. It was odd for him to call. There weren't too many things he could talk about with me—Ty was the only one of us still in the SEALs who would have had the security clearance. *Did something happen to my brother?*

"Jaxon." Mark's voice carried a hint of unease.

The alarm I'd felt at seeing who the caller was increased in volume. "Is Ty all right?"

"What? Yes. Sorry, that's not why I'm calling."

I gritted my teeth, waiting for him to get to the point. The weight of Kayla's safety pulled my nerves taut.

"We have a problem, and since this is in the jurisdiction of military police now, I can share a portion with law enforcement. We found the leak."

"Who is it?" It had to have been local, someone on the run, for him to be able to talk to me about it.

"It's internal. There was an investigation—we weren't sure who it was from, and we were all under suspicion. But there were some discrepancies in an email, and the investigative team determined the leak to have come from Malina's computer."

Ty had a thing for her. When they were around each other, the tension between them was palpable. It would hit him hard. "Let me guess. She's missing?"

"Yes."

I squeezed the bridge of my nose, thanked Mark for the heads-up, and disconnected. I would have to find out who led the investigation on our end, and I would eventually. My main concern was how Ty would react when he came home.

21

KAYLA

On the balcony and with a glass of Merlot in hand, I waited for Jaxon to get home from work. I'd finished painting the family room and the kitchen, which were open concept. It looked good. The colors my parents picked out were light and beachy, with an undertone of pale blue tinting the white paint. The trim was a bright white, highlighting the walls and giving a refreshing feel to the room.

They would move in two weeks, and I had to finish packing their place. I planned to have Jaxon take me there that evening for a few hours. Years of living would be hard for anyone to box up in a timely fashion, but with Jaxon helping, we could knock it out quickly. He was efficient and organized—yet another thing I loved about him.

I leaned my head back, letting the not-too-distant sound of the ocean help to slow my increased pulse at the realization of the depth of my feelings. Honestly, it was nothing new. I'd loved him my whole life. First, as my brother's best friend and someone I looked up to, followed immediately by years of crushing on him. I had wasted a lot of time, blaming him for the magical night we'd spent together and Kieran's accident. We'd gone from intimacy to grief, building a chasm between us rather than coming to one another in support. But the devastating news of my brother's death had blindsided us.

Through everything, I'd always loved Jaxon, and I was finally mature enough to face the mistakes we'd made with optimism for a bright future where we were together.

I glanced at the time on my phone. He'd called twenty minutes before to let me know he was on his way home. I'd made lasagna, which was not long out of the oven and cooling on the island.

In a few short days, Jaxon had once again become my world, and I was more than fine with that. The sound of the door opened, and he called out that he was home. It made me laugh. "Out here!"

"You made dinner." He grinned as he stood in the open doorway, leaning against the frame.

When I turned to smile at him, I caught the tension around his mouth and the corner of his eyes. There was a stiffness to his shoulders, despite the casual pose. Something must have happened, news that worried him. Whether it was work or Roy, I couldn't be sure. It wasn't about my cooking dinner. He and my brother used to beg me to make them grilled cheese sandwiches when we were young. I had a knack for making them all kinds of ways, something Jaxon did in adulthood, probably for old times' sake, a longing for what was. I got it. There were many times I did the same.

I got to my feet, set my wine glass on the table between the two lounge chairs, and went to stand before him. Rising on my toes, I pressed a kiss to his mouth. "I'll get us plates. Why don't you sit out here and relax?"

I would give him a few minutes to process whatever it was, to decompress. He'd tell me what was bothering him. If not, I would ask. We'd had too many secrets between us, and it wasn't the time to continue that practice.

I grabbed him a beer and a plateful of lasagna. Depositing them in his hands, I picked up mine and the Caesar salads then joined him back on the lanai. We ate in silence, and out of the corner of my eye, I witnessed the play of emotions across his features.

"What happened?" My quiet words broke the stillness between us.

He shook his head, setting his plate down and running his hands through his short hair. "I found out today that the woman Ty works with is wanted for treason. She's suspected of leaking sensitive information."

"Is Ty still out of the country?"

"Yeah. I don't know when he'll be back. There hasn't been any additional information about the hostages missing from the US Embassy in Venezuela." His hands tangled in his hair again as he hung his head. "Fuck. It's not good news, and Ty cares for her."

"I'm sorry." There wasn't much I could say. I didn't know the person he was talking about, but his brother... he was just as intense as Jax. All three of them were, in their own ways. Jax was the quiet, controlled one. Xander had more of an easygoing, carefree nature. And Ty was focused, driven, while also having the Hale charm in spades. He was a year younger than me, and I remember how much the girls in school would fall all over themselves for him, but I'd only ever been attracted to Jaxon.

I placed my empty plate next to his, and when I went to stand by his side, my hand gripping his shoulder, he pulled me onto his lap. With his head buried in the crook of my neck, we held each other. He breathed me in then told me what bothered him most. "I don't want to see him hurt."

"Are they dating?"

"Not that I'm aware of. They bicker like crazy. She acts like she hates him. Maybe she does. I don't know. There's just this intense tension between the two of them, and I've always wondered if there's more than meets the eye. It's hard to explain because Ty won't tell us much."

"Maybe the news won't devastate him then when he gets home?"

"With this information, I can't shake the fear that she's behind all the problems the SEAL team has had. The failed missions, the deaths… and Ty is on one now. If she causes harm to come to him—"

"Then you'll find her." His body was rock solid beneath my touch. Anger came off him in waves. The only way I knew to dissolve the turmoil was to put an end to the way he was thinking. Because I got it—he felt helpless. His brother was out there, maybe in danger. And Jaxon wanted to save him, to stop whatever had already been set in motion. That was who he was. But there wasn't much he could do.

We sat together, listening to the waves rolling, the cooling night air with the hint of chill teasing us. As his body relaxed, we chatted about mundane things, like the finished painting and when we would pack up his condo so he could move out.

"You know this was my last day at the station?" He grinned, and my heart swelled at how handsome he was.

"I do. Why do you think I made lasagna?" It was labor-intensive, but he'd always loved it when I cooked for him when we were kids.

"You get me."

I patted his washboard abs. "The way to your heart is most definitely through your stomach."

He chuckled, tugging at my hands, so I was lying against him again. "You've always held my heart, and it's not because of your cooking. But I'll take that too."

I sighed, content. "You're sweet to me."

"It's easy. I love you, Kayla."

My body heated as I caught his sincere gaze with mine. "I

love you too." We weren't holding back any longer. "You're it for me, Jax."

He threaded his fingers through my hair, then he shifted me so that we were facing one another, and I was ready for his kiss. The heat of it. The decadent passion. His touch was unhurried as he tasted and teased my lips. A whimper escaped. God, I wanted him. Always. When he deepened the kiss, tangling our tongues together, I was lost. Then found again with each swipe of his tongue and the teasing way he tugged my lower lip.

By the time we broke apart, our foreheads resting against each other and our breath mingling in erratic puffs, all the worries of the day had faded. He trailed a finger along my cheek until he cupped it with his palm.

Staying here with him outweighed everything except… there were things we had to do. I could spend hours in his arms in our bed later. Time was ticking, and my parents would return at the end of the weekend because my dad started back to work on Monday.

"More than anything, I want you to take me to bed. But I need to pack my parents' house up. I've only made a small dent."

"You want me to help?" He grinned, and my heart skipped a beat.

"Yes."

"You know I'll do anything for you." He pressed a lingering kiss to my lips before helping me to stand. "Why don't you put on jeans or something a little warmer, and I'll clean up the kitchen?"

I shivered as his hands left my body. It was cooler that night. There must have been a front coming through. "Sounds like a plan."

Getting ready didn't take long at all, and I shoved my phone —glad it was an older vision of the iPhone, so it fit—and the house key to my parents' place in my jeans pocket, not needing a purse, since Jaxon would drive. It would be a long night, but I was confident we would make a big dent in getting the house ready. And a part of me hoped that Kieran would be there too.

———

DESPITE HOW MUCH I longed to see my brother, to chat with him even if it was brief, he hadn't shown. Jaxon and I had spent hours there and were now on our way back home. Streetlights and headlights reflected in the puddles on the road as we drove back to his place.

Rain had been falling while we'd packed and continued in a steady rhythm. Inside the house and car, the staccato beat offered a cocooning effect. It was cleansing after the emotions of boxing up the living room, my bedroom, and part of the kitchen that wouldn't need to be used before my parents officially moved.

We'd made a lot of progress, and with another few hours of packing the next day, we would have the majority boxed and labeled, ready for the moving truck to come and haul it to their new home.

I was exhausted and couldn't wait to fall asleep in Jax's arms. He pulled into his spot in the building's parking lot. We both got out and were greeted with the excited yaps from Mrs. Malone's chihuahua. At the end of the isle, she bent at the back of a Mercedes, frantically trying to get him to come to her. I wanted nothing more than to go up to our place and pass out, but one look at the worry and frustration on the older woman's face tugged at my heart. "Maybe you should go help?"

"Yeah. I'll be just a second, then I'll come back and carry the boxes." Jax jogged over to her, and I rounded the back to look at how many trips it would take for the stuff from my room. I'd brought it because we were going to move everything in his condo to his other home on his family's island at once. It was easier that way.

A strange antiseptic smell came from Jaxon's side of the car, and I peered around. A shadow loomed over me. Sheer terror locked me in place for precious seconds. Then Roy was beside me. Flight took over. As I whirled, mouth open to scream, he clamped a rag over my mouth. My struggles lessened trapped against his body. Black spots crowded my vision. I tried not to breathe from the fabric he held over my mouth, but it was futile. I guessed what it contained. I couldn't hold my breath any longer, and chloroform filled my lungs. Then everything went dark.

JAXON

I'd left Kayla by my Escalade, exhaustion evident in the drooping of her eyelids as she leaned against the bumper. The succession of ear-piercing barks from Mrs. Malone's chihuahua propelled me to her side. Stooped over at the end of a black Mercedes, the elderly woman tried to coax her dog from beneath the car.

"Need some help?" I grinned as she turned her pinched face my way. The dog was making her ears bleed too.

"Please." Exasperation colored her words as she huffed. "I don't know what's gotten into that ragamuffin."

She was such a character. I dropped to my stomach and peered under the car. Milo was in attack mode with his lips pulled back, teeth bared, and ears pressed to the sides of his head. I followed the path to what Milo's nose pointed at. *Goddamn.* The sight of a very large, hairy spider almost had me rolling away.

What would a bite from a tarantula do to a small dog? I couldn't imagine anything good. Murmuring to the dog, I crept closer so that my arm could slip beneath the car and get close to Milo. The barking continued, despite me trying to calm him. I stretched as far as I could, and when my fingers curled around Milo's scruff, I inched him backward and away from the threat.

I kept my gaze locked on the spider, ready to forgo the slow retreat for a hasty one, should the tarantula move even a fraction of an inch. Several harrowing seconds later, I had the dog cleared from beneath the car, hugged him to my chest, and stood. I backed Mrs. Malone away from the Mercedes then escorted her to the elevator and passed her the dog when the doors opened.

Her thanks fell on deaf ears, literally. I waved off her appreciation and breathed out a sigh of relief when she and the dog were safely on their way to her condo. There was no need to freak her out and tell her what Milo had been after. I would put a call into maintenance when Kayla and I were upstairs.

I jogged back to my SUV, where Kayla had looked like she was about to fall asleep on her feet. When she wasn't leaning against the back bumper, I assumed she'd lain down to wait in the back, with the doors closed to shut out Milo's horrid yapping.

I opened the rear door. Everything in me stilled—she wasn't there. A sense of foreboding about how the tarantula got into the garage washed over me. A quick scan showed she wasn't anywhere in there. I rounded the open trunk to see if she had taken a box and snuck behind me and into the elevator while I was occupied with the dog. The boxes appeared untouched. My blood turned to ice. I shoved aside the panic and went into tracking mode.

Her ex had to have gotten in there somehow. I did another sweep of the interior, looking for clues. I found evidence of Roy's presence a couple of vehicles over. There were minute scratches on the window's rubber from a jimmy on the unlocked Explorer's back door. The back windows were tinted and would have obscured a large man lying in the back, waiting for the right opportunity, and Milo's barking had provided the perfect cover.

My fingers curled around my phone as I climbed behind the wheel of my SUV then quickly called in the abduction. The more of us out there looking for her, the better. With a click of the tracking app I'd installed on Kayla's phone, I turned the engine over and reversed, racing out of the garage to follow the moving dot on the screen.

Window down, I slapped the police light on the roof for the advantage of weaving through the cars on the roads at high speed. There was no doubt in my mind that I would catch them. Then that fucker would pay.

He better not have hurt her. My focus narrowed. I moved in and out of traffic. To keep batter watch, I slapped my phone into the holder mounted onto the dash. When the dot remained in place, I increased my speed again. If he realized she had her phone, there was no way he wouldn't dump it. I was damn lucky that he hadn't done so immediately.

In a sea of brake lights and squeezing tires, I searched for any sign of her.

Images of her smile, her laugh, and how she felt so right in my arms invaded my mind. I ruthlessly shoved them away as I careened around another corner, cars pulling over in haste as I put my foot to the floor for the straightaway. There was about a mile separating us. I was catching up.

The dot stopped moving, and I took another turn at a speed that almost rolled the Escalade. They were a couple of blocks ahead. My fingers gripped the steering wheel tightly. When I was on top of the location, I slammed on the breaks, drew my gun, and was out the door. Nothing stirred. They were supposed to be right there. I was in front of the Hawaii National Bank, but no one was in sight. I swept the perimeter.

The dot hadn't moved. My worst fucking nightmare was

that I'd lost her, just as I had her brother. But with Kayla, it was so much worse.

And then I saw it—her phone. I jogged a couple of feet to retrieve it. The screen was chipped and cracked from being tossed from a car. *Goddammit!*

They could have been anywhere. There wasn't a clear path to where Roy was headed while I was following him. While I didn't know him, I knew his type. Not far from the police station, I got back in my truck and sped away. I needed to take a look at the file on her coworker, Stephanie. My stomach clenched with a combination of rage and fear. I had a hunch Roy would recreate some part of her murder—with Kayla as the next victim.

23

KAYLA

y head throbbed, it felt like cotton filled my mouth,
and I tasted something slightly sweet. I lay curled on
my side. *Why is the bed so hard?* Confusion swirled as I blinked,
trying to clear my vision. The scent of disinfectant, like what I
would smell in a hospital, brought my memory back in a rush.
The shadow. Turning then having the cloth smother my
mouth. Roy.

White-hot fear filled my body. I took inventory. I was lying
on something very hard. Possibly the ground. There was a
damp, fishy odor that saturated the air. I had to be near the
ocean.

It was dark, but I couldn't see the stars or the glow from the
city. I blinked to clear the fog that filled my mind, and more
shapes came into focus. I was inside. The smell and cavernous
space that I could see clicked with something I'd seen on TV
about how Stephanie was found. When they'd pulled her from
the water, she'd been close to a fish-processing warehouse.
Roy's plan for me couldn't have been clearer, but I held out hope
that he hadn't brought me to the same place. My ears strained to
pick up any noise or hint of a threat.

I felt for my phone, panic curling my fingers when I discovered my pocket was empty. *Did I have it long enough for Jaxon to get a location? Could it be here, or did Roy toss it somewhere?* I hoped with everything in me that he hadn't thrown it away when he grabbed me, even though that was the most likely scenario.

The air conditioning hummed. In slow increments, in case he was close by, I shifted. I wasn't tied up. My head continued to throb, but it seemed to be from the drug, not an injury. I had to escape.

I rolled to my feet and crouched. The lights clicked on, blinding me. My hand flew up, shielding my face. Frantically, I blinked to adjust to the change. There. Between my parted fingers, I spotted Roy leaning against the far wall. Dread sat heavy in my gut. We were in a fish processing warehouse.

"I've been waiting for you to wake up." He shuffled closer. "Who the fuck was the guy, Kayla?"

"N-N-No one. A friend of my brother's." My gaze darted around the warehouse. *Is this where he'll kill me?* He didn't need a weapon. He was one. My neck remembered in great detail the slow squeeze he'd applied, the bruises, and the mirrored image of them on Stephanie's body. I stood, inching back with each footfall of his as he closed the distance between us. "It was a place to stay. He's like another brother," I lied, doing my best to sound convincing because I recognized the violence in his eyes that was seconds from exploding. "Why?"

He paused in his approach, weighing my words and testing them for the lie they were. When some of the outrage left his stormy gaze, I let myself breathe again.

"Why what? Why did I come for you?" His deep, gravelly voice sent another wave of shivers along my body.

I had to keep him talking. I didn't know his endgame, but I suspected it wasn't anything good. "Yeah." That was great. I mentally rolled my eyes. *Way to go, Kayla.* "What are you going to do with me?"

That sinister grin he graced his boxing opponents with changed his face from handsome to evil. I'd witnessed it many times in the ring. Nothing good ever followed that expression. The mindset that took him over when he fought was brutal and twisted, and he always won. I shivered.

"We're going to play a little game." He closed the distance between us, his hand reaching for me, and I smacked it away, jerking back. "You're going to tell me where the flash drive is, or I'm going to hurt you."

His hand shot out, and beefy fingers curled around my wrist. I was yanked forward before I could even react. *Oh shit!* The heat of his body seared me but failed to ease my spiraling panic. I wracked my brain for something to say that would appeal to him to be lenient with me.

"I was jealous. I would never do anything to hurt you," I lied in a desperate attempt to get him to stop. My free hand was flat on his chest, pushing without results. He bent to my neck and inhaled. "That woman you were with, and then the thought of Stephanie, too, pushed me over the edge. I wanted you all for myself."

His grip loosened a fraction. "The numbers girls never mean anything. They're there to use so when I come home, I can go slow and appreciate you."

Sick fuck. But I forced my revulsion to hide beneath parted lips and what I hoped were softened features. "Why didn't you ever tell me?" I patted his chest. "That's sweet, baby." Internally, I gagged on every word. But it was play the game or die.

"I don't need to explain myself."

The anger was back, the caveman effect in control. I had to work harder to diffuse it any way I could. "I just meant that it would have helped me understand. I wouldn't have been so jealous if I knew how much you cared, that you only wanted the best for us."

His hand moved down to my ass, and he squeezed. His

pupils dilated, and I shuddered but not in a good way. "Where's the flash drive?"

Crap. "It's back at our place. I hid it. I couldn't stand knowing you kept something of hers."

The indulgent chuckle and the satisfaction over how I was acting appeased his ego in a way begging wouldn't have. He thought I was simple, a doll. "Steph tried to run. No one runs from the champ."

"I never should have, baby," I cooed. "I didn't understand what we had. The sacrifices you made for us."

He kneaded my ass, and I fought from whimpering at how rough he was. There would be bruises, making it painful to sit tomorrow—if I survived. *I will.* There was no room for doubt. I had to convince him.

"I was going to kill you here, but I could be persuaded not to."

Christ. He'd always liked those cat-and-mouse games. I despised them and didn't want to play. But the stakes were my life. I didn't have a choice.

"You'll have to pay the price for your behavior. There are lessons and rules you will not break."

I forced myself to continue to suppress the fear and hatred from my face. I didn't know if it worked, especially with the tight way he held me to him. Relaxing my free hand against his chest, I rubbed it in circles instead. "Of course, Roy. We can work this out. Why don't we go somewhere so we can talk? It's gross in here. Not very romantic."

A calculated gleam flashed in his maniacal eyes, and I knew that even if I had him with my pseudo-acceptance, his plans weren't benign. "We can do that. You owe me, and it's time to pay up." He wrapped one meaty arm around me, locking me against him. The other left my wrist and fisted the back of my hair in a stinging grip.

When his mouth took mine in a punishing kiss, I tempered

my reactions and softened. Tears stung the back of my eyelids, and I tasted blood from his cruel handling. I fought the bile that threatened to climb my throat. It would be over soon.

Seconds felt like too many minutes before he released me from his abusive kiss. Satisfaction bled from his deep chuckle. "We'll have to go over the rules."

I didn't trust myself not to tell him to go to hell, so I nodded instead and thought of the beach, of a calm ocean rather than the tumultuous emotions warring inside of me. *There has to be a moment for me to escape. I'll stay vigilant. And maybe Jaxon will find me.* If I could get Roy to take us somewhere easy for Jaxon to locate us, even better—and that would be his condo. "I'm ready. Let's go home, Roy."

It wouldn't be that simple. I'd experienced his punishment firsthand, and I'd left because of it. I hoped things wouldn't escalate until my moment arrived to get the hell away from him. He made me wait as the gears turned slowly in his head. When he finally nodded, I knew I'd won a stay of execution, probably not for long.

No matter what, if we stayed there, he would kill me. Because I had a horrible suspicion that it was where Stephanie spent the last horrifying moments of her life.

His hand stroked a rough caress over my cheek. "Tonight will be fun."

He locked me against his side as he turned toward the warehouse door, and I shivered in fear and repulsion. My lungs could expand enough to breathe shallowly under the grip that kept me tethered to him. In a partial drag where my feet barely touched the cement floor, he maneuvered us to the steel door.

When he pushed at the door, releasing the locking mechanism, I gasped. I never expected there to be anyone on the other side—especially not Vivian.

24

KAYLA

"What is this? A happy reunion?" Vivian sneered.

"What?" I couldn't even. I stared at her, dressed in black yoga pants and a stretchy hot-pink T-shirt. Her blond hair was in artful waves around her shoulders, and her makeup was impeccable. It always was. *But what the hell is she doing here?*

Roy's confused expression matched my own, but he snapped out of it first. "Out of the way."

He probably thought it was one of his groupies, following him around. But it was late at night. We were exiting a fish-processing warehouse on the harbor. Sure, there were bars and restaurants around, but having her at the door like that... Nope, something wasn't adding up. I didn't care, though—*she can help me.*

"Vivi, let Jax know I'm fine. Roy and I made up, and we're going home." My gaze dropped to her hand, which had slipped inside her purse. *Is she going to call him now? That wouldn't be good.*

Roy growled and moved to push past her. "Move." He didn't even spare her a glance. She was an annoying gnat, just another groupie that didn't hold his interest—he didn't deem her important to furthering his career. His hand bit into my waist as he crowded Vivi.

"Not so fast." She pulled a gun from her purse and pointed it at Roy. "Back inside."

Roy tensed. He was going for it. She lowered the weapon and squeezed the trigger. There was a loud bank. My mouth fell open, and I jerked as he yelled then dragged me with him as he hobbled back a few steps. Blood oozed from a wound on his leg. When his arm loosened, I inched forward. Vivi shook her head in a slow side to side. "You too. Back inside."

She pushed the gun into his stomach. "Now. You move, and I shoot. Again."

We eased back. Roy was fast, but her finger was on the trigger. Even if he managed to knock the gun away, the probability of her shooting him before it cleared his gut was too high. Face red with fury, he obviously came to the same conclusion. "What do you want, crazy bitch?"

The door shut behind Vivi, and we backed farther into the warehouse. I wanted to know the same thing. Something wasn't adding up.

"That's a broad question. What I wanted for my life didn't happen because you men are all alike. You think with the wrong head. So what I want is for you to do something for me."

She wasn't making sense. "How did you know we were here? Did you call the police?"

She snorted. "You're so naïve. I shot him. Do you think I would have done that if I'd called the cops?"

Roy growled.

I glanced at his leg and the blood that dripped to the floor. He'd been through multiple rounds of beatings in the ring before he became an undefeated champ. My money was on him taking her. I didn't know Vivi's game. Stoking the fire was as good an idea as any, and I turned my attention to him. "I can't believe she shot you. Are you all right?"

He grunted.

"Since both of you are too dense to figure it out, here's the deal."

I ground my teeth. God, I hated her. She hadn't changed one bit from when I knew her in the past. She was always such a bitch when she hung out with my brother's crowd. Then poor Mateo let her get her claws into him.

"You've been asking too many questions, Kayla, and Mateo's on my case about it. I've got a mediocre life going here—not the one I should have had, but it is what it is at this point." She shook her gun at me for emphasis, and I crowded closer to Roy. "I've kept an eye on you, and when your boyfriend pulled out of the garage, I figured it was worth a shot to follow. Lucky for me, it paid off. But—"

"You get off on watching?" Roy interrupted, his interest piqued.

"Shut up, Neanderthal. I know this place. They fished that reporter chick outta the water here. I did my homework. She dated you. You've got Kayla here. It was perfect. Two birds, one stone. Why the hell didn't you finish her off?"

"She's—"

"That was rhetorical. I don't care." Her lips sneered back. "But you are going to choke her. End her. Now."

25

KAYLA

"You want him to kill me?" My mouth hung open, and I snapped it shut. I should have known she hadn't changed. "What the hell, Vivi?" Fortunately, I knew Roy well, and he didn't answer to anyone.

She rolled her eyes and tossed her mane of blond hair over her shoulder. "Of course, I want him to. But nothing has worked out the right way since we rolled your brother."

I took an involuntary half step back, feeling as if she'd punched me in the gut. "What are you talking about?"

Roy shifted at my side. It was subtle but enough to alert me to his intentions. He would never save me—he would save himself. I worked to keep her attention on me. "You rolled Kieran?" I couldn't even process what she meant by that.

Then he sprang forward. The gun went off. Someone screamed. A second passed, and I realized it was me. I clamped my mouth shut.

She shot him again. It was loud—final as the warehouse amplified the sound. Tears rolled down my cheeks. Roy lay in a hump at Vivi's feet. I couldn't see where she'd shot him, but his head had jerked back. He was facedown, and the wound wasn't visible—nor was the vacant stare that I imagined was in his eyes. For that small favor, I was grateful.

The cold from inside the room invaded my bones. My entire body convulsed. I couldn't stop shaking. "W-What?" I shook my head, trying desperately to regain control. "W-Why?"

A slow smile spread over her thin lips as she stepped over Roy's lifeless, hulking form. "Why the hell not? Your boyfriend was a risk. If he wasn't killing you, chances were high he'd come after me after I interrupted. No matter. I'm capable of seeing this through."

After several shuttering breaths, I got myself under enough control to stop my teeth from chattering. I took another step back, trying to maneuver toward one of the large vats that held shaved ice when the fish were harvested and brought in from the boats. If I could dive behind it, find something to throw at her, I might stand a chance. "I don't understand. Why would you want to kill me? I have nothing to do with your life. I never have."

"No. Not back then. But your brother did. You know, I tried to get him to notice me. To dump Leslie." A dreamy sigh paused her words. "He was going places. But when he flat-out rejected me, it became clear he was an obstacle. That was when I fully committed to Mateo. But I couldn't let it go, not completely. Your brother stood in the way of the life I wanted."

"How?" She was insane. I inched back another half step. I couldn't take my eyes off her—or stop wondering why the place was so clean. The panic that had been so close before tested the fragile bonds that held it at bay. I felt them slip. She was going to shoot me. I couldn't see a way out.

"How did your brother stand in the way of the life I wanted? Deserved?" She shook her head, and that fanatical, unhinged gleam came back into her blue eyes. "Oh, honey. My Mateo should have gotten that full ride that your brother stole out from under him. Mat was the top pick at the University of Hawaii when your brother declined."

Oh God. "But Kieran changed his mind."

"At the last minute. Yes. They bumped Mateo to second string, since he hadn't committed—that was on him. We had words over it. Then they went with Kieran instead."

I had never understood Kieran's change of heart, but the pregnancy made it make sense. At the time, I hadn't cared because he would be closer. We were all happy about that.

The pieces of Vivi's craziness were falling into place, and horror held me in its embrace as I waited for her to confirm what I'd come to know in my heart: the second shark's-tooth necklace, the picture of the guys all hanging around Mateo's car, which had been the same car Mateo had said he'd gotten rid of shortly after high school. It had been evidence.

I could see no way out, and that was it for me—Vivi intended to clean house and sweep any piece of the past from the playing board.

26

JAXON

I headed into the police station to get Roy's address and check out the file on Kayla's coworker, Stephanie, to see if anything stood out and would lead me to where Roy held her. Someone called out to me. My foot was poised on the stairs, but I paused at the heavy weight that reverberated in the way he'd said my name.

Caught in his tone's snare, I waited. My instincts pricked at me to listen, despite the intense need I had for action. I couldn't waste a single second when it came to finding Kayla.

I pivoted. Beneath a streetlight in the parking lot, Mateo stood in front of his car's bumper, hands shoved into the pockets of his jeans. The laid-back, chill guy I'd known was gone. He looked as if he was facing a terminal sentence. *What the hell is going on?*

"You're looking for Kayla, aren't you?"

I gave a sharp nod, absorbing everything about his downtrodden demeanor, piecing together the cause for it and not liking where it was leading me.

His head fell back, and he closed his eyes. He forced out a

resigned breath. "I think I know where she is. I'll hop in your car and tell you everything on the way there."

Fuck. I hated to think of what secrets he might share. I would almost have preferred that he didn't. I wanted to go where Kayla was without any distractions.

Behind the wheel and on the road, Mateo told me exactly where to go. It clicked, then, and I called it in. The fish-processing warehouse was near where Kayla's coworker had been pulled out of the ocean.

As I put my foot to the floor and raced through the streets, Mateo recounted his story. "I couldn't lose her."

I bit my tongue as he filled me in enough to gain an understanding of her mental state.

All those years, the Kane family suffered pain, not knowing what had happened. It was time everything was out in the open. Her parents needed to know the secret Leslie and I held about that night and all she and Kieran had lost.

———

Kayla

A LOUD SQUEAK caused Vivi's attention to shift to the heavy steel door as it opened—it was my chance. I pivoted and put the metal storage bin filled with ice for holding the fish between us. She swung back and locked her beady gaze with mine. "Stop."

I froze. Mateo stood in the partially opened door. His hand was around the steel, keeping it from slamming shut. Regret shadowed his features, aging him and stealing the easygoing vibe he wore like a second skin.

"What are you doing, babe?" His voice was velvet soft.

"Tying up loose ends," she snapped, but a tremor ran through her hand, and the gun briefly wavered. "She wouldn't leave it alone… asking you about that night, about the car. I couldn't let her steal more from us."

"Kayla's never taken anything from us. Let her go." He reached his free hand toward the gun.

Vivi shook her head. "No. First the scholarship—"

"You ran Kieran off the road?" I couldn't stop the words from tumbling out. Mateo turned to me, and I swear he'd aged a couple of years.

"Vivi and I'd gone to the point. We were drinking. Upset about the change in circumstances. I'm so sorry, Kayla. Your brother—"

"Ruined everything!" Vivi shouted. Her body shook with rage. "Everything was so clear that night. Leslie told me they were coming to the point. But they were late. When I spotted their car on the curve, it was the perfect opportunity. It was fate."

Mateo winced.

I had to know. "You weren't driving, Mat?"

With a tiny shake of his head, he told me he wasn't. "But I might as well have been. I wanted to come forward. Kieran was my friend. I loved him like a brother."

"Shut up." Vivi snapped. "He wasn't good enough to be your friend. That position was yours, a guarantee to get picked up for the NFL—"

"Stop." Mateo's voice cracked like a whip and shut her up. "I was good but not good enough for the NFL. Kieran was. I didn't have the delusions you did. Please give me the gun, Vivi. It's over."

She shook her head with tears running down her face. "I can't, Mat. I have to protect us. What we have."

"What we have is built on a lie, and I don't want it anymore. Not if you hurt Kayla too." Mateo moved closer to her, the door still in his hand. *Why is he doing that?* Then I saw the reason: Jaxon.

Our gazes caught and held. An air of control surrounded him. He motioned down. I sank to my knees while Mateo continued to argue with his crazy wife, unnoticed by the two. But I had to watch. I wouldn't have been able to handle it if Jaxon was shot.

Mateo moved forward, the door wide. Jaxon slipped behind him then around in two seconds flat. Vivi didn't even get a chance to scream. Jaxon disarmed her and had her in flex cuffs before any of us knew what had happened.

Then he was by my side, helping me to my feet. I threw myself into his arms. The horror of why my brother died replayed in my mind. "She killed him for a spot on a football team. For the possibility of Mateo getting drafted for the NFL."

Cops poured into the building while Jaxon held me. Vivi was taken outside and to a waiting squad car. The blues and reds flashed in the dark and painted the walls with each opening of the door as more officers secured the scene.

Mateo, his hands bound behind him, convinced one of the officers to let him have a word with me. They stood off to the side but close enough so that we could talk. I had the side of my face pressed against Jaxon's chest, but I met Mat's gaze, waiting to hear what he so badly needed to say.

"I'm sorry, Kayla. I loved your brother. When Vivi slammed into his car, I had already consumed most of a bottle of Jack. I was barely conscious. When she got control of the car and kept going, I—well, I never saw what she'd hit. Everything came together when I found out your brother was in a fatal car crash. I wanted to go to the police. Vivi convinced me not to. And I was scared. Then there was the other night. When she over-heard you asking questions at the bonfire, I knew she wasn't going to let it go. I'm sorry I wasn't here sooner. I'm glad the truth is out. His memory deserves it."

It meant something, his confession. In time, I thought I'd be able to forgive him. I couldn't say anything as Mateo was led away by Matheson.

Jaxon kept his arm around me as we walked out, skirting around Roy's body to exit through the open door.

27

KAYLA

Jaxon and I were back at his place, but I didn't remember the drive home or going inside the condo. I vaguely remembered talking with my parents on the phone. Jaxon had taken it from me to tell them I was okay and that we would see them soon.

I was wrapped in a blanket and tucked into his side, and the two of us cuddled together on the couch as the numbness faded. The TV was on in the background, and its low murmur added comfort. I shifted in his arms, and our gazes met. "Thank you." It needed to be said. He'd come for me.

A sad smile curved his lips. "I'll always be there for you, Kayla." He tucked a strand of hair behind my ear. "You're my life. There was no other option."

I couldn't help but voice my fears over those last few seconds before he had arrived. "I didn't see any way out of it. I couldn't reason with her." My body shook. "There are so many regrets. All those years I wasted being mad at you… I blamed you for keeping something from me about Kieran because I could feel the secrets between us, see them swimming through your eyes. And I couldn't bear to have anything about him withheld. And I don't know, maybe it was also a maturity thing." I took a stuttered breath. "We'd only recently found our way back to each other, and Vivi was going to end my life. It wasn't fair."

"There aren't any more secrets. I'm sorry I didn't tell you Kieran would elope with Leslie or about the baby. His loss—their loss—was so devastating. I didn't want to add that to the grief you already shouldered."

"We can't do that ever again." Tears filled my eyes, the pain of losing my brother swimming beneath the surface of my fragile control all over again.

"No more secrets." Jaxon's vow flashed in an ironclad determination in the strong set to his square jaw and in the steel that swirled in his gaze. "I love you more than I can ever say, Kalya. Let me show you just how much for the rest of our lives."

He smoothed the pad of his thumb over my trembling bottom lip. I needed him. Tilting my chin up, I parted my lips in invitation. He didn't disappoint. The caress of his mouth was drugging. When he slipped his tongue inside to tease and torment, I melted against him.

Unhurried, he stoked the heat that was always between us to a slow burn—just what I needed. When he broke away and rested his forehead against mine, our breaths mingling, warmth had soaked from him into every inch of my body. He'd fed me some of his energy, chasing away the worst of the shock of the night. *I—we—will be okay.*

"Do you want to move to the island early?" he asked gently. "The painting is done here. The only thing left to do is pack up and settle in over there."

It was tempting, but I didn't feel right about it yet. "No. Let's wait until my parents have moved. Another week or two isn't long, and I want to be here for them. It's going to be painful when they learn about everything that happened."

"Your dad already knows."

Of course. He was the police chief, and Jaxon had talked

with them when I couldn't say much more than that I was okay. "Let's spend tomorrow with my parents. We can help them pack up the house fully and lend a hand when they move. Then we can start our lives on your family's island."

He grinned, and another flame of heat unfurled in my stomach at how handsome he was. "You do know we're only a twenty-minute boat ride from seeing them?" He tweaked my nose. "We'll bring them breakfast tomorrow and stay as long as you want. Tyler is keeping his condo here in Honolulu for all of us to use whenever we want. We can sleep there after your parents are settled here. Until you're ready to go to the island."

I laced my fingers with his and squeezed. "That's perfect. Thank you." Once they were situated and weren't reeling from the loss of Kieran all over again, we would move too. I didn't want to abandon them. I looped my arms around his neck and smiled. We would be okay—I knew it.

Jaxon turned toward the TV. Something had caught his attention. I loosened my embrace and snuggled back into his side to see what it was that had locked his emotions behind that impenetrable wall of the soldier he was and always would be.

A bar of red slashed the TV's bottom portion with Breaking News stamped across it in white. An image of a Black Hawk filled the screen. Four people made their way from the helicopter, tired, unkempt, and sandwiched by several Navy SEALs.

They were the remaining hostages. But it wasn't until Jaxon spoke that I realized what was wrong.

"There are only four of them. Five were still missing, and where is my brother?"

KAYLA

My toes curled in the foamy surf as the first rays of the sun reflected off the rolling ocean waves in a glistening display. It was peaceful, with only a few surfers to the north end of where I stood. Stephanie's article about Roy had run that morning. Another would follow, regarding his death. With that chapter wrapped up, I was free to go anywhere I wanted. The funny thing was, I was where I should have been all along.

I wound my arms around my waist from the slight chill to the morning, waiting for the sun to chase it away. The scents of ocean and spice and a hint of coconut mingled with sand and surf, drifting on the warm tropical breeze. "I miss you, Kieran," I whispered, hoping my words would find a way to reach him.

"I'm never far, Little K."

Out of the corner of my eye, my brother towered over me, looking hale and happy. "I popped in on Leslie today. She had her baby. A boy."

Pain and happiness warred in my heart. "That was supposed to be you guys, all those years ago."

A sad smile curved his handsome face as I turned to him. "It was." He brushed a tear from the corner of my eye, tingles following in the wake of his feather-soft touch. "You know everything now."

"I do." I ached for what he and Leslie had and lost.

"Don't worry about us. Leslie and I will find each other again, in another life. I'm happy for her. The last thing I would want is for her to be alone. She deserves to be loved, to have another baby." He chuckled. "She's been sending leis into the water in hopes that I'll come back to her. Those damned flowers came back every time. She knew I was close, even if she couldn't see me."

Leis were typically made of plumeria flower, a flower chock-full of meaning. Not only did the flower indicate whether the wearer was single or taken by which ear it rested over, but the sweet-smelling flower was cast in the ocean in hopes of loved ones returning. Long ago, when ships sailed, a lei was set adrift in the water. If it returned to shore, the vessel would too. If not, all those lives would be lost in the ocean.

The meaning behind why Leslie was tossing the fragrant, velvety petals in the water wasn't difficult to decipher. She'd harbored hope that my brother would somehow return, even if only in spirit, which he had.

I would call Leslie later and wish her and the baby well. "Did she know that you were there at the hospital?" The surf swelled and kissed the side of my foot, only to roll back again.

"For a moment. It was enough."

Chills danced over my exposed skin, raising the fine hairs in its wake. She would have recognized the same scent that I did. Of course, she'd known he was there. How difficult it must have been for her to date, get married, and get pregnant again—moving on. I drowned in Kieran's warm brown eyes, forcing myself to surface and ask the hard question I needed an answer to. "The baby."

"Our baby was a girl." Kieran glowed with joy. "I've held her, seen her."

I nodded, another piece of the past settling.

"Tell Jaxon he's right where I want him to be. And if he hurts you, I'll be back to haunt his ass."

I laughed, shaking my head but glad for the levity. "I love you, Kieran."

"I love you, too, Kayla," he whispered, his deep voice mingling with the rolling surf and breeze.

When I blinked, he was gone, but I felt him in my heart, and everything was lighter. The grief became less oppressive, and I knew I would be okay.

"What are you doing out here so early?" Jaxon's arms came around me, pulling me against his chest as he nuzzled my neck.

I reached behind me, linking my hand at his nape and burying my fingers in his hair. "I needed a few moments alone with Kieran."

He turned me in his embrace, concern swimming in the complicated depths of his brown eyes. "Are you all right?"

I dropped my gaze to the sand, and Jaxon did the same. Next to me were footprints—*Kieran's*. There was only one set, so very much bigger than my feet. The imprints in the sand didn't come from any direction or lead anywhere. They just were.

Jaxon stilled, his arms tense around me. And for a moment, we were both lost in our thoughts.

"Kieran said I'm where I'm meant to be. And if you hurt me, he'll be back to haunt your ass."

Laughter burst from Jaxon's mouth, followed by the grin he'd worn around my brother. It was wolfish and full of mischief. The two of them were trouble. God, I loved that man. "It figures that he's still trying to control my life." He winked at me before dropping to a knee, my hands in his.

"What are you doing?" My heart beat against my ribs. That

scent from before, of ocean, spice, and coconut, intensified, and I felt my brother's presence rather than saw him.

"This seems like the right place and time, with Kieran nearby."

My hands tightened on his, and I waited for what he would say while my heart pounded against my ribcage.

"You are my world, Kayla Kane. I fell in love with you when we were kids and never fell out. The first time we tried to be together didn't work out for us, and you slipped from my grasp. This time, we're doing things right. I want to go to sleep every night with you in my arms and wake each morning to the sight of your beautiful face. Each day is a new opportunity to share our hopes and dreams and to build the life we both want. Marry me, Kayla. Make my dreams come true."

Tears rolled down my face, and I laughed, happiness spreading through every inch of me. "Yes." The wind whipped my hair around my face as Jaxon stood and tucked the long, dark strands behind my ears.

He wrapped me in his arms, holding me tightly against him. Then his mouth came down on mine, and time stood still. One touch from him, and all was right in my world. I knew that together, our lives would be everything I'd ever hoped for. I couldn't wait for our next adventure.

The End

Continue reading the Deadly Isles Special Ops series with Forged by Secrets:
https://amymckinleyauthor.com/deadly-isles-special-ops/
Keep reading for a sneak peak of Fake Fiancé: A Second Chance Office Romance.

Keep up with Amy's releases by joining her newsletter:
http://eepurl.com/dEBqJn

FAKE FIANCÉ

A SECOND CHANCE OFFICE ROMANCE

———

Adeline

A SENSE of heaviness hung in the air as I sat at the small folding table my best friend Eileen had set up for the psychic. I waited in silence across from her, shifting in my chair, unsure what to do as this was my first time meeting, let alone talking to, a medium. We'd already exchanged hellos, and I wasn't about to offer up any details about who I was. Instead, I passed the awkwardness by studying the woman before me.

Long waves of black hair surrounded a face of indiscernible age. I couldn't pinpoint it—twenty-eight, thirty-five, or older? Small laugh lines framed eyes and mouth set in an olive-toned face that maintained a youthful quality, but her eyes—those were ancient.

Downstairs, the sound of music and laughter from the small party in our sorority house carried on. That was where I wanted to be—enjoying the excitement of a carefree night with my friends, celebrating all we've accomplished. Instead I was upstairs sitting across from a woman I didn't know, who was supposed to connect me to people who had passed. I fought the urge to twist a lock of my hair and instead twined my fingers in my lap. I didn't know why I was so nervous.

It was supposed to be fun.

Chills ran up and down my spine as she leaned forward, her bracelets clinking. Mysterious obsidian eyes reflected something otherworldly that I couldn't define or understand. I wanted to rub my arms but clasped my hands tight instead. Electricity charged the air, and all the fine hairs on my body stood on end.

I wasn't having fun.

Seconds ticked by, then on an inhaled breath, she slowly blinked, a soft smile curving her full red lips upward. "Adeline, interesting name." Her gaze turned introspective. "Your mother is with us."

I fought the urge to stand up and walk away. But the fact that she knew something about my mom kept me in my seat. I craved hearing anything about her, even if this entire thing wasn't real. I missed her terribly.

"She says she named you appropriately. Someone in your family tree had the name Adeline, but she died… at sea." Her eyes remained unfocused, and she tilted her head as if listening to someone whisper in her ear.

"I don't understand what you're saying. I'm supposed to die at sea?" As I waited for her answer, I shifted in my chair, unsure what to think. Mom had been into our family history before she passed, but I wasn't. I barely remembered who that person was that shared my name. I'd thought Mom just liked it.

"No, nothing like that. Your mother says she's proud of you."

I jumped as the psychic's voice pierced my thoughts of Mom.

Proud of me. That was something I knew, and it was rather generic. My skepticism returned in full.

Mom died years ago from cancer, leaving my father and me to figure out our suddenly strained relationship. Not going to lie and say it was easy—it was anything but. Promises were made before Dad, too, passed away.

A soft smile curved the psychic's face. "She says she has no regrets."

Maybe. My parents were happy, blissfully so, despite the hard times, lack of money, and failing business. "But you gave up being a model when you met Dad. You were on a path for success." I couldn't help it. I spoke as if Mom could hear me. I wanted to believe she could.

"She says, 'That wasn't the life I wanted. I wanted a family. There wasn't a day that I regretted marrying the love of my life. But you, my darling daughter, have a different path. Follow it and find your happy.'"

Even said in the medium's voice, that would have been something my mom would have said. Chills danced along my bare arms, and I wished I'd worn something over my threadbare "I run because I really like beer" T-shirt. Emotions were too close to the surface, and tonight I didn't want to succumb to them. I was starting out on a new adventure, and so were my friends. Mom was right, even though leaving was bittersweet, I wanted to "find my happy." I didn't feel as if it was here.

Relaxing back, I decided not to take myself seriously. The experience should be at least interesting, even if I weren't having a great time. I gave the woman a slight nod. And really, I wasn't positive I believed in what she was saying, part of me thought it could be my deep desire to connect to my mom, to hear her words and feel her presence, even if only for a few minutes.

The rational side of my brain rejected that this woman could actually connect with the dead. As for the medium knowing my name, Eileen must have told her, no big deal. She could've researched all of us at the party on the internet and learned that my mom died.

"She's insisting you follow your heart, that you need to leave the area."

"Why?" I couldn't resist. I'd planned to skip town on the heels of my college graduation, which was tomorrow. There wasn't anything holding me here. Not Tommy, that was for sure —despite the plans he had for us.

The woman tilted her head, her gaze once again turning inward, and a faraway look eased the lines in her face, taking years off her thirty-something appearance. "The neighbor isn't the one. She says your father is with her and regrets pushing you. She's pointing to…" Her eyes sharpened, and my back snapped straight. "You're a designer? No, that's not what she meant. There's an inn and a man that owns it. You're to go there."

"I'm flying out the morning after graduation. Did Eileen tell you this?" My voice held an edge of skepticism I couldn't hide. Business tycoon Stone Crenshaw recently bought a hotel in Italy, expanding his New York-based business to Europe, and I'd applied for the position of executive assistant. With my multiple summer jobs, helping my dad on the office end of his construction company, business degree and internship experience through another of Stone's hotels, I was qualified. And apparently, he was desperate.

Thanks to my sorority connections, I was able to get pushed to the top of the application list and recommended by his current assistant, and sorority alumna. Again, the psychic could have heard about this from anyone in my sorority.

The medium smiled and tapped the table with a long copper-painted nail. "You will have success there, in time." She tilted her head to the left—her go-to move before she dropped something weird on me—her dark eyes narrowed, and the smile fell away. "Wait."

A frown deepened the grooves around her mouth, and my heart skipped a beat. I toyed with the Saint Valentine pendant worn on a silver chain around my neck. The "in time" comment about my success concerned me a little. Obstacles weren't unusual, but I was determined. I would change my lot in life. I would not be destitute like my parents or trapped as my mother was to a man she loved so much she gave up her budding career. She'd always said she didn't regret it, but I think a part of her had. Why couldn't she have had both the man she loved as well as a career?

"There is another here." The room chilled. "So insistent."

I swore the air crackled with electricity while phantom fingertips danced along my arms, and I shivered.

She shook her head. "Hmm. He's agitated. I can't quite understand him. But this name, it's important. Cristiano Santoro." Her brows scrunched, and she leaned forward slightly. "Oh… your mom is back. She's adamant that you look him up."

A wave of sadness washed over me, the likes of which I hadn't felt since we buried my mom. That name. Tears formed and rolled in rapid succession down my cheeks. *Dammit.* Either his name had triggered me or the continued talk about my mom as if the medium actually saw her.

I swiped the wetness from my face and shoved the unwanted and unexplained feelings aside as best as I could. Strangest few minutes of my life. The pressure in the room eased. Another of my sisters noisily came up the stairs and leaned against the doorjamb. The medium flashed me a smile before her focus shifted away from me. I thanked her and slipped past Monica, my sorority sister, who was anxious for her turn.

I made my way back to the main room and shed the odd sense of déjà vu, welcoming the rather loud music that poured from the stereo in the corner. Josie handed me a drink as I stepped off the last stair. I spotted Eileen near the back wall, sitting on the couch with Lauren. When Eileen saw me, a shriek shattered the last of my tension before she launched herself off the cushions at me.

Laughing, I returned her hug before she pulled back, squeezing my shoulders. "So? How was it? What did she say?"

I plastered a smile on my face, determined not to ruin this for her. She'd set it up with me in mind, even though it was an event for all our sisters. She knew I was missing Mom so much more after Dad passed six months ago. It'd been a tough semester. "It was…" I couldn't help it. I had to know. "Did you tell her about my mom? Or that I was leaving after graduation?" Not everyone knew, and I'd thought Eileen had kept that information to herself. I was supposed to share my news about the job with them tonight, after the psychic finished. Maybe Eileen had told one of the other girls in the house.

"Nothing. She knows the first name of each one of us like what's on the sign-up sheet, and that's it." Her brows furrowed, and her fingers tightened on my shoulders as worry pulled her features taut. "I haven't told anyone that you're leaving the day after tomorrow."

"Maybe it was Tiffany then." That was the name of the alum sorority sister I'd contacted about the job. She was a few years older than us, had graduated four years ago, and worked in the position that I'd be taking over for Stone Crenshaw.

Eileen shrugged. "Maybe? But I don't think so. Everyone here wants the time to be about them. I don't think they're even thinking about what you'll be doing next." Her mouth compressed in a thin line. "Why? Did she tell you something about your new job?"

"Sort of." Pulling out my phone, I typed the name she'd given me into my notes app to check out later. "Not much. My destiny is supposed to be there, whatever that means."

"Ohh, what if you meet the man of your dreams? I mean, it is the city of love." A hopeless romantic, Eileen flashed me a wide grin while her shoulders shook in silent laughter. She knew I didn't share her fairy-tale views. "Maybe you'll find your very own Romeo in Verona—the place where Romeo and Juliet were."

"Shut your mouth. And their relationship ended in tragedy. I would have to be crazy to wish for that. Besides, you know my goal is a career. No man will distract me from achieving that."

She rolled her eyes. "Not what I meant. I wasn't referring to Tommy, but a real romance, minus the tragedy. You don't need a linebacker hinging his football success on you being present at his games. You did break it off with him, right?"

I bit my lip thinking about the best way to answer her. "Yes. I told him the other day."

Eileen narrowed her eyes. "How did you tell him?"

Crap. "In text."

"You can't be serious."

"What did you expect me to do? He never listens to me when I tell him I don't want to be together. I gave him back the ring, and this way it's in writing. He can revisit what I'd said. Besides, I'll be gone soon. It'll all work out."

"If you say so." Eileen shrugged. "Back to Italy and your prospects there. What I'm not talking about is Romeo and Juliet —but the fact that you'll be working alongside a gorgeous man." She nudged my shoulder. "And with this to-die-for, long silvery-blond hair, those eyes, and your rack..." Her finger circled the air between us and wiggled to include all of me. "Well the whole drop-dead package, he won't know what hit him." She glanced at my gym shoe-clad feet. "We better have you practice walking in heels."

I snorted at her absurd description and worked to shake off the cloak of anger that'd settled around me at the mention of my looks and meeting a man. Just the idea of using my appearance at the new job to land a husband reminded me too much of my father's outdated opinion and Tommy's pressure to get married before the NFL draft. We weren't even dating anymore. It wasn't real. I sighed, regret heavy in the knowledge that Tommy had followed me around like a puppy for our entire high school experience, then college, in a relentless pursuit.

We'd dated, sure, but I wasn't all that serious about taking the relationship any further than having fun at college. There was something missing. That spark I'd expected to feel and I know he hadn't experienced it either. And then later, when Dad fell ill… I'd only pretended Tommy and I were solid to my dad so he didn't leave this world worrying about me. But the truth was, I didn't need someone to take care of me. I'd been doing that ever since Mom died five years ago. Tommy had other ideas about that, and when he'd dropped to a knee beside Dad's hospital bed, I couldn't steal the pure joy that lit up Dad's gray features. Outside the hospital room, I'd set Tommy straight. I wasn't marrying him.

As to my looks? Eileen was high. Even though I sort of understood her point. I was young, and people were weird. But I wasn't anything special. Average. With my hair secured in a bun and professional clothes, no one would spare me a second glance. College was a cesspool of horny guys. It would be different in a business environment. I was sure of it. As for the heels comment, she may be on to something there. I never wore them.

"Let's get a drink." Distracting Eileen from her happily-ever-after fantasies would be easy with the mention of partying together.

She bounced on her toes, her curls mimicking each movement. "Yes! I'm so glad you decided to hang with us one last time before you go."

I rolled my eyes. "So much drama."

Eileen linked our elbows as we made our way over to the bottles of beer and wine. "You love that about me."

Debatable. But I would do just about anything for her. I shook off any lingering negative thoughts. Tonight wasn't for dwelling on the baggage I carried with me. I would leave it behind when I boarded my flight at the crack of dawn the day after we graduated, heading toward the future I wanted for myself. This time was about having fun with my best friend and sisters. They mattered. And after tomorrow, I'd finally be free to live the life I craved.

Chapter 2

———

Stone

AFTER SPENDING most of the night tossing and turning, sleep came in the early morning hours. Slumber's smothering embrace held me tight, dragging me into a dream that had replayed often since my arrival in Verona. A time long gone eclipsed the present, and I stepped into the life of another, no longer the hotel owner, but a busboy living with his father in the basement of this very building.

My arms laden with guests' luggage, I sidestepped a group of people checking into the hotel. My father was employed here, too, and happy with his lot in life. I was not. My dreams were bigger. This place, although extravagant, was not how I wanted to exist—fetching and carrying things for people with a better station than mine. One day, I vowed to make my fortune. I'd toyed with the idea of owning an inn. Perhaps not as grand as this one, but a successful business nonetheless.

"*Mi scusi.*" I maneuvered around a group of gentlemen.

That's when I saw her—a vision. Long, honey-blond hair artfully arranged with a few wavy tendrils around the face of an angel. My heart skipped a beat then sped up, thundering in my ears.

An older couple stood beside her. They paled in comparison, despite their similar build and facial features. Slowing my stride, I caught snippets of their conversation, discovering her name was Francesca. I tore my attention from her for a brief second to scan for a suitor, a husband. There was no ring on her finger, no man by her side. But everyone noticed her.

She looked to be of similar age to me, perhaps a year or two younger than my nineteen years. As if in quicksand, I forced myself to move forward, the burden of the luggage nearly forgotten. *Look at me*, I implored her with my thoughts.

When her brilliant blue gaze collided with mine, she froze. Lush lips parted on a gasp, and an enchanting pink infused her high cheekbones. She had to have felt the connection too.

Her stunning features seared into my mind. I had to talk to her. If only I could. One look at those around her made it clear that it would not happen, at least, not at this moment. But I was inventive. I'd find the perfect opportunity to steal time with her.

Everything in my being pulled me toward her. *She's the one.* I was sure of it. Electricity charged the air. I recognized this moment for what it was—one where everything would change. Destiny.

The shrill beep of my alarm screeched, and I jackknifed in bed, ruthlessly ripped from sleep. I scrubbed my face with the palms of my hands before taking in the deep-red chairs, dresser, and double wood doors all visible from where I sat on the four-poster bed. I was in my room at the hotel, my latest project.

It was just another dream. She wasn't real. Even though my heart beat sluggishly from the loss of Francesca's presence—from the possibility of her.

Even with the physical grounding of my room—the hotel I

owned rather than being employed in—I couldn't shake the haunting dreams, the vision of the girl, nor the chains of despair whenever I went anywhere near the basement. That, I avoided at all costs.

———

Continue reading Fake Fiancé: A Second Chance Office Romance, or check out more of Amy's books with Broken Circle, book one in the Gray Ghost romantic suspense thriller series.

https://amymckinleyauthor.com/standalone-titles/fake-fiance-a-second-chance-office-romance/

https://amymckinleyauthor.com/gray-ghost-series/

Hidden

Taken

Covert Recruits (coming soon)

Irina

Sasha

Zena

Nadia

Katya

Amy McKinley is the *USA Today* Best-selling Author of the romantic suspense thriller Gray Ghost Novels, Deadly Isles Special Ops, Covert Recruits, Moonlit Destination Series, the Five Fates paranormal romance books, and several standalone titles. Her edge-of-your-seat books are filled with surprising twists and just the right amount of heat and danger. She lives in Illinois with her husband, two daughters, two sons, and three mischievous cats.

You can find her at: www.AmyMcKinley.com

If you enjoyed reading BOUND BY SECRETS as much as I did writing it, I hope you'll consider leaving a review.

facebook.com/amymckinleyauthor

twitter.com/AmyMcKinley7

instagram.com/amymckinleyauthor

bookbub.com/authors/amy-mckinley

www.ingramcontent.com/pod-product-compliance
Lightning Source LLC
Chambersburg PA
CBHW071826190726

48292CB00005B/1631